THE JEWS

First published in 2016 by punctum books, Earth, Milky Way.
www. punctumbooks.com

ISBN-13: 978-0692620625
ISBN-10: 0692620621
Library of Congress Cataloging Data is available from the Library of Congress

Cover image: Alexander Grindberg, 'The Theatre of Meyerhold' (ca. 1920)
Cover design: Eileen A. Joy & Vincent W.J. van Gerven Oei
Typographic design: Vincent W.J. van Gerven Oei

NACHOEM M. WIJNBERG

the jews

Translated from the Dutch by
Vincent W.J. van Gerven Oei

punctum books

CONTENTS

MOSCOW

STALIN: Stalin.
BERIA: Cold?
STALIN: Stalin.
BERIA: Worried?
STALIN: Stalin.
BERIA: About what, Stalin?
STALIN: Jews.
BERIA: Which Jews, Stalin?
STALIN: Hitler.
BERIA: I don't know. I really don't know, Stalin.
STALIN: Jews.
BERIA: Yes, Stalin, I hear what you're saying. We're looking into it. It won't be long before I can tell you how the Jews managed to make Hitler abdicate. We're looking into it.
STALIN: Time.
BERIA: As soon as possible.
STALIN: Stalin.
BERIA: You don't need to worry.
STALIN: Jews.
BERIA: The commission of inquiry consists of Jews but they're under strict supervision.
STALIN: Jews.

BERIA: Of course there are many good Jews, Jews who are on our side, more of them each day.

STALIN: Jews.

BERIA: I do what I can. We're about to send secret envoys to Germany.

STALIN: Jews.

BERIA: Jews. Good Jews. The best Jews we could find, Stalin.

STALIN: Cold.

BERIA: It's cold, Stalin, I'll have it fixed.

STALIN: Jews.

BERIA: You're right. But rest assured. There's the commission to present its findings.

(The commission of inquiry files into the room, headed by the chairman.)

BERIA: The commission of inquiry has finished its preliminary report, Stalin. Would you like to hear it?

STALIN: Cold.

BERIA: You see. Stalin would like to hear your report fast. Let's get started.

STALIN: Jews.

CHAIRMAN: The Jews indeed, Stalin, you are absolutely right. Our inquiry is divided in three parts. The first part concerns a reconstruction, as precise as possible, of the events related to Adolf Hitler's abdication. The second part is an inquiry into the history of the Jewish conspiracy. The third part maps out the current state of the Jewish conspiracy. The first part has to a large extent been completed.

BERIA: Let's skip to the important part.

CHAIRMAN: By the end of 1934, Hitler's power was unchallenged. Toward the end of that year, just before Christmas, he announced on the radio that he had abdicated and that he had been succeeded by Martin Heidegger. As soon as Hitler had finished speaking one could hear the sound of applause. Then Heidegger started his first big radio speech. We have studied gramophone records of the speeches and it is beyond doubt that those were indeed Hitler's and Heidegger's voices. We didn't find any indication that Hitler may have been confused or drugged, either. The following day, Heidegger gave his second big speech. That is the one in which he nominated Walter Benjamin as Vice-Chancellor. According to reliable witness reports, Benjamin had been present at the conversations between Heidegger and Hitler during December. We do not know how often they talked. During this period, Benjamin also remained in constant contact with the other Jews, notably Adorno, Horkheimer, Marcuse, and a few others.

STALIN: Hitler.

BERIA: Stalin wants to know how they made Hitler abdicate.

STALIN: Jews.

BERIA: What the Jews did with Hitler, that's what Stalin wants to know.

STALIN: Stalin.

BERIA: Stalin wants to know whether this could also easily happen to him. That's what it's about. Continue about Hitler.

CHAIRMAN: Right after Christmas Hitler left for Munich. He had a house built nearby. At the beginning of the next autumn he moved into it. He had designed the house himself. During the construction, Heidegger and Hitler talked on several occasions. At the construction site and probably elsewhere too. Benjamin attended some of these conversations. Hitler was buried a year ago. Heidegger attended the funeral. We have a photograph of his face and also a photograph of him sitting alone for a while on a bench once the funeral had ended. We're unaware of Benjamin's whereabouts during the funeral. There are still many things that we don't know about the takeover. That's why we want to send two secret envoys to Germany. Male and female. Both Jewish. We hope that they will be able to talk with the German leadership.

STALIN: Jews.

CHAIRMAN: They will pretend to have fled.

STALIN: Jews?

CHAIRMAN: To gain trust.

BERIA: In Germany no one should worry about openly speaking to them about the Jewish conspiracy.

CHAIRMAN: A thorough preselection has yielded a capable male candidate. His name is Salomon Maimon. He is twenty-two years old. After being rejected from the theater academy he spent a year at the university. On his second attempt he passed the entrance examination successfully, but in his second year he was expelled from the theater academy owing to unsatisfactory results. For a while he worked as a cleaner. Then he worked as a puppeteer. He was granted a special exemption from the theater ban to give public puppet shows. Both his parents are of Jewish heritage. Among his mother's ancestors there is also a negro. He cannot read Hebrew but he knows a few blessings and short prayers by heart. A prayer can also contain one or more blessings. Separate blessings are said before someone obeys a commandment or eats something or sees something for the first time and in other circumstances of a similar nature.

BERIA: You don't have to explain about the Jews.

CHAIRMAN: Sometimes Maimon used the texts of these blessings in his puppet theater. May we call him in?

BERIA: Call him in.

COMMISSION: Salomon Maimon!

(Salomon Maimon enters.)

BERIA: You know why you're here. Are you comfortable? Are you Jewish?

CHAIRMAN: He is Jewish.

BERIA: Can he speak already?

CHAIRMAN: My apologies. Of course he can speak.

MAIMON: Yes, thank you.

BERIA: You have attended the theater school for a year?

MAIMON: In the beginning of the second year they expelled me.

BERIA: Stalin, this is Maimon.

STALIN: Maimon.

MAIMON: Thank you.

BERIA: You will receive a small role in history. Do you know why?

CHAIRMAN: I've explained it to him several times.

BERIA: The assignment is secret. You're not allowed to discuss it with anyone.

CHAIRMAN: He hasn't discussed it with anyone. For the past few months he has lived with me in my home and he has prepared himself for his assignment from early in the morning till late at night.

STALIN: Jew.

BERIA: You've worked as a cleaner?

CHAIRMAN: He worked briefly for the Moscow sanitation department until he got permission to give puppet shows.

BERIA: You swept the streets?

CHAIRMAN: No, he cleaned houses. When someone dies alone in his home, the city sends in cleaners to empty the house and to clean it up. Also the home of someone who dies in a hospital or prison and hasn't been visited by anyone.

BERIA: Let him speak for himself. Maimon, is it difficult work?

MAIMON: The houses of the dead are often very full. Sometimes it takes an entire day to throw away everything that needs to be thrown away.

BERIA: What is not thrown away?

MAIMON: Jewelry, watches, food that's still packaged, furniture and clothing if it still looks fine. Indoor plants if they're still alive.

BERIA: If a cleaner finds something that he could very well use for himself, can he keep it?

MAIMON: If it would be otherwise thrown away the cleaner can keep it.

BERIA: Have you seen many dead bodies?

MAIMON: I haven't seen any dead bodies. They are removed before the cleaners are sent in.

BERIA: He didn't make it at the theater academy. I'm sure he didn't mind that we have abolished theater.

STALIN: Stalin.

BERIA: Abolished for the moment. For the moment! In the world to come we will reintroduce theater and anyone who wants to, even mister Maimon, will be able to be a perfect actor.

CHAIRMAN: Stalin wants to give us the largest present, the world to come. During our lifetime we will be allowed to enter.

STALIN: Fish.

BERIA: No one has to do work that is embarrassing because someone else can do the work better but someone wants to give him something to do. Anyone who wants to can fish in the morning and hunt in the afternoon.

CHAIRMAN: Or the other way around.

BERIA: Do you always say what first comes to your mind?

CHAIRMAN: I'll try to speak more carefully. I thank you for your good advice.

BERIA: I didn't give you any advice.

STALIN: Stalin.

BERIA: The Soviet Union's theater was the best theater in the world. That's precisely why we abolished it. Sometimes a large disappearance is necessary to make space for what's coming. I am always curious about what has become of all those suddenly unemployed actors. If they're good at singing and dancing they sometimes work in film.

STALIN: Stalin.

BERIA: Carrying around giant images or statues of Stalin in parades is an obvious substitute for theater. Still, those parades only belong to the meantime.

STALIN: Stalin.

BERIA: Music film is the type of film most helpful for bringing the world to come closer. A music film is first shown to Stalin: as he watches the film they film his face. This film shows when Stalin is laughing, when he is looking worried or bored. The film of Stalin's face is sent to the director of the music film. The director is then able to adapt the film. Stalin likes music films in which the main actors engage in dancing contests and afterward no one remembers who has won. Stalin also likes dancing acts in which the dancers smoothly form figures together. For example dancers dancing toward and away from each other like an opening and closing flower. It works best when the dancers are dancing in the dark wearing glow-in-the-dark costumes, with small lamps attached to their heads and arms. But the most important aspect of the music film is the music. That's why it was difficult to make good music films before the invention of sound films. It's not always possible to rely on the pianist or violin player.

STALIN: Jew.

BERIA: Stalin always poses the right question. The pianist or violin player sitting below or next to the projection screen in the cinema making music while there is singing and dancing in the film. In small villages there is sometimes no one who is able to play an instrument and a blind beggar is asked to sing while the film is shown. It is easier to make comic films. A beggar walks down a street. Thousands of policemen appear at the end of the street. For a moment they stop. A policeman points at the beggar. The beggar looks at the policemen. Then he starts running. He runs through the street, the policemen running behind him. As fast as possible he peels bananas, throwing the peels over his shoulder. He stuffs his mouth with the bananas. He can't possibly eat any faster. Just in time he arrives at the edge of the city. The policemen aren't allowed to go further and are left behind disappointed. The beggar throws the last unpeeled bananas into the air, as high as possible. Who needs music if the jokes follow each other rapidly? But what do we need comic films for when we can make music films? Maimon, can you sing?

CHAIRMAN: He cannot sing. Should I have looked for someone who could also sing?

STALIN: Jew.

BERIA: Stalin is considering using the law of the Jews as the text for the latest comic film. To honor the Jews.

CHAIRMAN: How could the Jews be thankful enough?

BERIA: No one loves music more than Stalin. That's why

he is frightened when the German declaration of war is sung instead of handed to him on paper. Sometimes he asks for music in the middle of the night. Someone brings him a gramophone record, which he plays on repeat dozens of times. Sometimes he also calls a poet in the middle of the night. Next to his telephone he's got a list of poets' telephone numbers. Sometimes he calls a poet and says nothing while the poet says his name and repeats his name and listens intently. A large number of dead poets were also given telephone numbers. Also poets who died long before the invention of the telephone. They are on Stalin's list. They've also been listed in the Moscow telephone directory for a year.

STALIN: Music.

BERIA: The very first music film is about a young woman coming of age in the countryside. When her mother sees how beautiful she has become she travels with her daughter to the city. They buy new clothes and every evening mother and daughter visit the theater. In the theater the daughter is spotted by a high-ranking judge who asks her to marry him. She says: this is the beginning of my life. After the wedding she lives in a large mansion, far from the city. She flees. In the city she dances at parties and in restaurants. She breaks all the glasses. First she asks politely: may I have your glass? Later she takes the glass without asking and throws it to the ground. A man drinks from one of the shoes in which she's danced. Suddenly she screams: they invented sound; who will want to marry me now?

CHAIRMAN: I saw the film together with my wife. She couldn't stop crying.

BERIA: She likes films that she can cry about?

CHAIRMAN: She also likes films about animals.

BERIA: Since the invention of the sound film all films about animals are music films.

CHAIRMAN: I hope you don't mind when I say that my wife preferred comic animal films.

STALIN: Jew.

BERIA: Is it difficult to become a Jew?

CHAIRMAN: Very difficult.

BERIA: Seems you've been lucky, Maimon, don't you think?

CHAIRMAN: He's been lucky.

BERIA: Maimon, do you know what your great-grandfather looked like?

MAIMON: I don't know what any of my grandfathers looked like.

BERIA: If I held a photograph of a great-grandfather in my hand, would you want to see it?

MAIMON: It is a photograph. A face like any other.

BERIA: A face with your mouth. I'm talking about the father of the father of your mother. He traded in clothes and he was a beggar. His son, your grandfather, no longer traded in clothes but in oil and fat and he was a beggar. You great-grandfather lived in a village. There were two other Jewish families living in the village even poorer than your family. The non-Jews appointed your great-grandfather as the one responsible for the Jews in the village. When a poor Jewish traveler passed the night in the village and left early in the morning without paying for his lodging and food they would pass your grandfather the bill. When a Jewish traveler died in the village your grandfather would pay the costs of the funeral. One day a large number of Jewish travelers arrived in the village. Maybe seven or eight and they were all poor. Some of them looked sick. Your great-grandfather locked himself in his study. He closed all the curtains and locked the door. He told his wife to tell the neighbors that he had left the country. Your great-grandfather was rich, your great-grandmother was goodlooking.

CHAIRMAN: His great-grandfather wasn't particularly rich.

BERIA: I've once seen a great-grandmother looking better than his. He has his great-grandmother's ears.

MAIMON: A face with my mouth, another face with my ears, so what? Please excuse me for saying so.

BERIA: Of course, but say I had a letter from your great-grandmother.

MAIMON: It's a letter.

BERIA: The letter is written to your grandfather, your mother's father.

MAIMON: To him, not to me.

BERIA: Shall I read you the contents of the letter? Would it really not move you at all to see the paper and your great-grandmother's handwriting? Your great-grandmother writes to your grandfather that he shouldn't give up begging, even if he were as rich as the richest man in the country.

CHAIRMAN: He's a very young man, he hasn't developed a sense yet for these sorts of things like you and me. On a free evening there is nothing I would rather do than read my parents' and grandparents' letters and look at their pictures.

STALIN: Jew.

BERIA: Maimon, are you prepared for your assignment?

CHAIRMAN: The members of the commission have prepared him as well as possible. We have taught him how to unexpectedly take a lengthy pause in a conversation and occasionally laugh softly without an obvious reason. He's also able to sit in a chair in a relaxed way.

BERIA: Can he shut someone up with his hands?

CHAIRMAN: We thought that wouldn't be necessary for his assignment. Moreover we didn't have enough time for that.

STALIN: Time.

BERIA: Stalin does have a bit of time to teach him. Maimon, watch closely. We don't have time for something complicated. Hardly anyone ever has time for that. Two punches. Stalin?

STALIN: Time.

BERIA: The punch to the throat and the punch to the stomach. Both are enough to make someone shut up.

(Stalin gets up from his chair, positioning himself in front of Beria. With his clenched fist he makes several punches toward Beria's Adam's apple, without touching him. Then several punches in the direction of Beria's stomach. Then in quick succession with his right to the throat and with his left to the stomach. Beria doesn't move.)

BERIA: Did you get it, Maimon?

CHAIRMAN: He's got it, Stalin.

MAIMON: Thank you, Stalin.

STALIN: Time.

BERIA: Time is on our side.

STALIN: Time.

BERIA: If Stalin had had more time he would maybe have taught you the knee between the legs.

CHAIRMAN: Stalin is always short of time.

STALIN: Stalin.

CHAIRMAN: Stalin?

BERIA: Stalin is not a king.

CHAIRMAN: I'm not used to standing so close to Stalin.

BERIA: Stalin isn't afraid to dream the same dream every

night.

CHAIRMAN: Of course not. My apologies.

STALIN: Jews.

BERIA: Do Jews dream?

CHAIRMAN: Not often. I couldn't tell you when was the last time I woke up and remembered a dream.

BERIA: Continue with your report.

CHAIRMAN: We have also found a suitable female candidate. Natalia Goncharova was taught by the rabbi of Birobizhan. She's twenty-five years old, finished the theater school, and then went to work at the city theater of Kiev. No lead roles but nice supporting roles. After the theater ban she worked as a saleswoman in a shop.

STALIN: Jewess.

BERIA: Soon Jewess.

CHAIRMAN: Already Jewess. She's already a Jewess. Just before I arrived I received a message from the rabbi notifying me that she was already a Jewess.

BERIA: Nothing happened to her, right?

STALIN: Jewess.

BERIA: Young Jewess, already.

STALIN: Good?

BERIA: She is very convincing, very good. She easily evokes emotions, in large numbers at the same time.

STALIN: Kiss.

BERIA: Herds of emotions, Stalin.

CHAIRMAN: She's waiting outside.

BERIA: But Stalin can rest assured. Maimon won't be carried away by his feelings. He won't be distracted from carrying out his assignment. Maimon?

CHAIRMAN: He has a great natural disposition not to be carried away. And he's also received additional training. She's been trained and tested too. During the final weeks we have put them nearly every day in circumstances in which they could panic or be overwhelmed by pity.

BERIA: You have tested them for weeks? Stalin can put his trust in them? They have an important assignment. Are they aware of this? Maimon?

MAIMON: I know that the assignment is important.

BERIA: When Stalin will have made the world to come begin, someone may abandon himself to love in the morning and to anger in the afternoon and to pity in the evening. How large does something have to be before it reminds you of Stalin?

CHAIRMAN: As large as the world?

BERIA: If Stalin died, what should be the size of his grave?

CHAIRMAN: Before or after the beginning of the world to come?

BERIA: Do you think that's a good question? What would you write on Stalin's gravestone? Here lies Stalin?

STALIN: Kiss.

BERIA: Stalin wants to know what she looks like.

CHAIRMAN: She's already waiting. She can enter directly.

BERIA: Stalin's asking what she looks like.

CHAIRMAN: Very well. We have seen her. Her lips don't need honey.

BERIA: Can you be a bit more precise?

CHAIRMAN: Her lips don't need honey, even if they have been kissed to pieces.

STALIN: Kiss.

CHAIRMAN: I haven't kissed her. None of us has kissed her.

STALIN: Time.

BERIA: Unfortunately Stalin doesn't have time to see her.

STALIN: Not see.

BERIA: Stalin prefers not to see her. But she has to be good. If she isn't everything could fall apart. Do you understand?

CHAIRMAN: We understood so. She is truly very good.
STALIN: Not see.

(Stalin gets up, walks away. The commission bows and waves him goodbye. Maimon waves too.)

CHAIRMAN: Stalin is a sensitive man.
BERIA: Call her in.
COMMISSION: Natalia Goncharova!

(Natalia Goncharova enters.)

BERIA: Come in.
CHAIRMAN: Come in.
BERIA: You're nearly a Jewess?
GONCHAROVA: Last week the rabbi said I was ready.
BERIA: Fine. The rabbi knows what he's talking about.
CHAIRMAN: She's a Jewess.
BERIA: I think it would now be good to leave both of them alone.
CHAIRMAN: The commission would like to recite the end of its preliminary report.
BERIA: Is it brief?
CHAIRMAN: A few lines.
BERIA: Alright.
CHAIRMAN: Who wants to speak?
COMMISSION MEMBER: This is the history of the Jewish people as rabbits. Blood transports heat to the ears where it disappears through the skin into the air.
CHAIRMAN: That's it.
BERIA: Warm Jews?
CHAIRMAN: Slightly colder than yesterday but still warm and sunny. In the middle of the night maybe a refreshing

thunderstorm and a brief rainshower. The next morning again bright and warm.

BERIA: Is that a Jewish joke?

CHAIRMAN: My apologies. That wasn't my intention. Honestly. I don't know why I said such a thing.

BERIA: Where's your joke now?

COMMISSION MEMBER: He could hit himself on the head like an alarm clock.

(Beria leaves, followed by the chairman, who is followed by the other members of the commission. Goncharova walks up to Maimon. They sit down next to each other on the floor.)

MAIMON: A calm kiss to the knee?

GONCHAROVA: The rabbi told me that the kiss is allowed.

MAIMON: Always?

GONCHAROVA: Is that a trick question?

MAIMON: A question. He was never taught by a rabbi. Does the other have to be awake when you kiss the knee or can the other also be asleep? Is it allowed to kiss the other awake?

GONCHAROVA: You've really never taken any classes?

MAIMON: Not from a rabbi. When I was a small child five or six older men would visit my parents on Saturday afternoons. They would sit at the dinner table and my father would join them. My mother brought them a plate of cookies and something to drink and then left them alone. One time my mother unexpectedly came in to get something she had left in the dining room. Suddenly they all fell silent and looked at each other as if they weren't sure whether they were allowed to do what they were doing. I would often stay in the dining room playing on the floor underneath the table. My father had a big old book. He would put the book on the table and open it. The open book was passed from one to the other and each time one of them would try to read a few lines aloud. But they read it word by word and for many of the words they didn't know the meaning. Later they usually left the book unopened on the table. Sometimes one of them would bring out a newspaper and they would discuss the contents. I never heard them talk about kissing.

GONCHAROVA: You can also calculate it. One afternoon the rabbi taught me how do to it. It was a dark afternoon. Outside it was dark and quiet. There was a plate of cookies on the table. The rabbi told me that his wife had made them early that morning. The door to his room was left ajar but I didn't hear any sounds from the rest of the house. His jester wasn't there either. The rabbi told me he was sorry about this because his jester was actually very good at calculating.

MAIMON: Calculate what?

GONCHAROVA: Whether a kiss is good. Instead of explaining it you can also calculate it. The rabbi says that you may only do it as a joke, not seriously. You take two of the most indispensable components of the kiss that you want to calculate, for example "mouth" and "knee" and you transform each word into a number by giving each letter of the word a numeric value, adding them together. Then you add the two words and check by which number you can divide the sum without remainder. You try the numeric value of the jewels: wisdom and victory and understanding, and of the seven other jewels. If you can divide the sum by "victory" then the kiss is not only allowed but also glorious, if you can divide by "understanding" it is understandable.

MAIMON: What is a kiss to the knee?

GONCHAROVA: I don't know every kiss by heart. Besides,

if the calculation doesn't work, you can also add numbers until it's possible to divide their sum. For example you add the number of "hand" because you grab the leg with a hand before kissing the knee, and if that doesn't work you can also add "leg" or "thigh." You shouldn't take the calculation too seriously. It can be relaxing after a whole day of hard study. The number method is a method of explanation but that method itself should not be understood too literally. The method may hide an explanation but the calculation results may not. The rabbi said that I can also use the calculation method to improve my acting. If I'm allowed to play a certain role I can write down the character's most important qualities and calculate the numerical values. If I want to know whether a certain action fits that character I can calculate whether the action can be divided by a quality or a sum of a number of qualities. If I'm sure whether a certain action fits the character and the calculation doesn't work, that offers a good reason to recheck the list of qualities and maybe change it.

MAIMON: What do you look like?

GONCHAROVA: Why do you want to know?

MAIMON: Tell me what you look like. Relaxed? Tense?

GONCHAROVA: Depends.

MAIMON: Convincing? Grotesque?

GONCHAROVA: Not often, I hope.

MAIMON: When did they ask you to do this?

GONCHAROVA: A long time ago. I don't remember when. I've known the rabbi even longer. I visited him for the first time with a few classmates, when we wanted to perform a Jewish play.

MAIMON: Which Jewish play?

GONCHAROVA: A short comic play that we had to invent ourselves. You never had to perform Jewish plays? I've performed dozens. Meyerhold calls together several students and says we're going to perform a Jewish play. He usually has a few props with him. For example a broom or a folding ladder. Then he says: what can three Jews do with a broom and a folding ladder?

MAIMON: I never took lessons from Meyerhold.

GONCHAROVA: We performed a Jewish play but it didn't work. Every time Meyerhold walked away to get a new prop. At the end of the day the floor was littered with props but we still didn't know what to do. Meyerhold suggested that we visit a rabbi to ask him how Jews behave when this or that happens to them. For example when the sky darkens and they hear a distant thunderstorm. Meyerhold phoned the rabbi to announce our visit. After supper we went to the rabbi's house. In the rabbi's study there were a table and a chair. There were no bookshelves but the floor was filled with stacks of books. Two portraits of Stalin were hanging on the wall. Hanging between the portraits was a cardboard sign with the names of the ten jewels written in large black letters. The rabbi was friendly and patient. His jester was there too. When the rabbi tied his shoelaces the jester untied his own before retying them. When the rabbi smiled the jester started to laugh out loud. One of us asked the rabbi to show us his way of studying. The rabbi sat down at the table, an open book in front of him. The jester squatted on the table, next to the book, and moved his head and his hands as if playing a violin. He began to hum out loud. Someone asked the rabbi what he looks like when he's sad or desparate. The rabbi said that he couldn't show that without prior preparation. But the jester immediately began to jump up and down in a squatting position, pulling out his hair. He also banged his head against the tabletop. The following day we told Meyerhold about our visit and he said that he wanted to meet the rabbi and his jester together with me. A week later I accompanied Meyerhold on his visit. That was my second time.

MAIMON: I attended the theater school only for a year. In that year I was never allowed to play a Jew.

GONCHAROVA: We hadn't phoned ahead but the rabbi let us in at once. He opened the door himself. His wife wasn't home. The rabbi took our coats and put them on a chair in the hallway. A male voice asked who had come in. The voice came from the study. The rabbi said to Meyerhold: That's my jester. In the study Meyerhold asked the rabbi to demonstrate his way of studying once more. The rabbi returned to the table with his book and the jester climbed on the table with his invisible violin. Then Meyerhold asked him to show what he looks like while praying. The rabbi got up, took his prayer shawl from the closet and wrapped it around his shoulders. The jester got behind him and jumped on his back. The rabbi moved his upper body back and forth, slowly and carefully so as not to shake off the jester. Meyerhold thanked the rabbi profusely and gave the jester a small note with his telephone number. Later the jester called him and he acted in a number of shows. He also played in the very last show on the evening before the theater ban was put into effect. He played Stalin's mother. Didn't you attend the final show?

MAIMON: Should I have been there?

GONCHAROVA: I lived in Kiev at the time but I came to Moscow especially for the final show. Didn't Meyerhold invite all his former students? It was a beautiful show. Meyerhold played Stalin. The play had been written especially for that one show. It contained many long speeches. Stalin's speech from the balcony of the Winter Palace. Stalin's speech at Lenin's burial. Stalin's speech at the opening of the new court building in Moscow. The play ended with Stalin's speech when he issued the theater ban. Once the play had ended the actors didn't return to bow for the audience. We cheered and applauded but the curtains didn't reopen. When I was standing in line at the wardrobe I saw the jester passing by. He was still wearing his costume and hadn't even taken off his make-up. I raised my hand but he didn't see it or he didn't recognize me. For the last months I've met the rabbi twice a week for my lessons but he no longer had a jester.

MAIMON: They asked me only a month ago whether I wanted to do this. Only this morning they told me you would join me.

GONCHAROVA: They had told me about you before. Happy?

MAIMON: Everything that's divisible by happy.

GONCHAROVA: Doesn't sound happy.

MAIMON: Why does it have to be calculated? Why isn't a happy kiss just called a happy kiss? Did the rabbi tell you?

GONCHAROVA: Two weeks ago I visited the rabbi for the last time. At the end of the day the rabbi got up and asked me to join him outside. He didn't walk to the front door but to the garden door at the back of the house. The sun was setting slowly. The sky had a color between red and purple.

MAIMON: Not a cricket chirping, not a frog croaking.

GONCHAROVA: A day is good because you can see when the day has ended and a new one is beginning. That's what the rabbi says.

MAIMON: Kiss to the knee?

(The commission enters. It is carrying a canopy, holding it up above Maimon and Goncharova. Maimon gets up and reaches out to Goncharova to pull her up.)

COMMISSION: A big kiss.

CHAIRMAN: A kiss to kiss someone who has dropped from someone's arms and is helped to get up.

COMMISSION: A kiss, a kiss!

GONCHAROVA: How does one kiss differ from another?

COMMISSION: Kisses linked to a certain time or not, kisses linked to a certain other action or not, kisses made necessary by a certain other action, kisses making necessary a certain other action. There are many ways to make a difference.

MAIMON: Why one difference and not another one?

CHAIRMAN: As much difference as necessary.

COMMISSION:

Contradiction.

How to solve it?

Make a difference

That solves the contradiction.

Is any difference allowed?

Man and wife He makes them.

Who knows of a difference

So unexpected?

CHAIRMAN: A good difference!

COMMISSION MEMBER: She moves her neck.

CHAIRMAN: Her neck.

COMMISSION MEMBER: Her breasts.

CHAIRMAN: Like impeccable young animals.

COMMISSION MEMBER: She wants to touch him with her

breasts.

CHAIRMAN: Underneath her clothing they are moving toward him.

COMMISSION MEMBER: How many breasts?

CHAIRMAN: Who counts breasts?

COMMISSION: Please take another breast; who counts breasts?

CHAIRMAN: Maybe this is enough about breasts?

COMMISSION MEMBER: He looks as if her breasts are on fire.

CHAIRMAN: As if she's keeping text between her breasts.

COMMISSION MEMBER: Her skin.

CHAIRMAN: At night her skin keeps her groom awake.

COMMISSION MEMBER: Her lips.

CHAIRMAN: Her eyes.

COMMISSION MEMBER: Her belly is soft.

CHAIRMAN: Her mouth.

COMMISSION MEMBER: Her tongue carefully moistens her lip.

MAIMON: Kiss?

CHAIRMAN: Good boy. The groom tries to act like a lion.

COMMISSION MEMBER: Like a lion.

CHAIRMAN: Not rude but still impatient. The groom doesn't need to rip the bride's clothes from her body but he has to make it clear that he cannot wait.

MAIMON: Like a lion?

CHAIRMAN: You may smell her.

GONCHAROVA: Me too?

CHAIRMAN: Certainly. You may smell each other. That's an old custom. The boy and the girl meet each other in the girl's parents' house. The boy is invited to sit next to the girl, for example on the couch. The girl's mother pours tea, the girl's father talks with the boy. The mother asks the boy how much sugar he takes in his tea. One by one she drops the sugar cubes into the tea cup. The boy says the blessing over the tea. Then the girl's father and mother talk with each other as if they were alone. Sometimes they get up and walk to a far corner of the room. Or they leave the room nearly closing the door. The boy and the girl may unintentionally bend over and smell each other. Like a lion and lioness.

MAIMON: Smell what?

CHAIRMAN: He begins by smelling her hair and her neck. She tries to smell his hands.

(The rabbi of Birobizhan enters.)

RABBI: Are you ready for the wedding?

MAIMON: Should we have prepared ourselves?

RABBI: Someone who can marry and isn't married can marry immediately. Did you wash your hands?

MAIMON: Immediately?

CHAIRMAN: They can marry. They're old enough.

COMMISSION MEMBER: How old is old enough?

RABBI: The groom has to be happy when he holds or kisses the bride. He may not look sad or disappointed. Even when there's no third party.

GONCHAROVA: Who's the third party?

MAIMON: Stalin?

CHAIRMAN: Stalin is a third party?

RABBI: I was sitting in the underground train. The train had stopped in one of the beautiful stations that Stalin had constructed. A man and a woman got into the carriage and sat down opposite of me. I greeted them by nodding my head and smiling and asked the man something. The man responded briefly and immediately posed a new question. I didn't have to choose between speaking with an unknown woman or being impolite to an unknown woman and maybe embarrass her. At the next station I got out.

CHAIRMAN: He doesn't look sad or disappointed. They can marry immediately.

RABBI: Where is the glass?

(A member of the commission takes a glass from the pocket of his jacket and places the glass on the floor. Each of two other members also take out a glass but put it back. The canopy wavers. The members of the commission put the canopy down.)

RABBI: The glass is because of the love that the Jews have invented.

GONCHAROVA: Jewish love?

CHAIRMAN: Promise love.

RABBI: Each promise leads to more promises and why wouldn't someone keep his promises? Or: each promise redeems promises that haven't even been made yet. He and she are sitting at a table in a restaurant. A violinist walks up to the table and plays a melody that would remind them of each other had one been far away from the other. She asks: what are we celebrating?

CHAIRMAN: And he says: we are celebrating you. Then they walk in the moonlight holding each other's hands. The non-Jews see the Jews doing this and start to imitate them. Now they've been doing it for so long that they think they invented it.

MAIMON: The Jews invented that?

RABBI: The non-Jews have bed temples. You shouldn't think that a bed temple resembles a brothel.

CHAIRMAN: He is too young to have visited a brothel.

RABBI: He was a small child when the last brothel was closed down.

CHAIRMAN: A brothel is a badly lit place in a badly lit part of town. In front of a brothel's entrance there's a man in a suit that's too small for him. In the brothel's main room there are women waiting for their visitors. The visitor dances with one of them. The visitor and the woman hold each other's hands. The visitor's other hand rests on her waist, the woman's other hand rests on his shoulder.

RABBI: Bed temples don't resemble brothels. On a holiday a man puts on his best set of clothes, has breakfast with his wife, and is seen out by his entire family on his way to the temple. Animals, too, happily watch him go. At the temple gate the man delivers his gift of grain or oil. Then a priest leads him inside. The priestess has taken a bath and has anointed herself with oil immediately after drying herself. She has put jewelry around her wrists and her ankles and neck. She has drawn warm kohl around her eyes. She's lying on an elevated platform covered with freshly cut grass. Late in the afternoon he returns home and he embraces his family members one by one and also his slaves so they can smell the temple.

CHAIRMAN: The Jews indeed need to invent something else. A man like the rabbi of Birobizhan would invent another two or three forms of love without a problem.

RABBI: The temple is a large building. It looks like a station of the underground train. The stones of the outer wall are alternately dark red, bright green, and deep blue. The high priest is a tall and stately man with the rectangular beard. His white clothes are washed every day, even if that day he didn't touch a sacrificial animal. The road toward the temple is loaded with Jews and their animals. Sometimes the Jews stop and it takes fifteen minutes or half an hour before they are slowly able to move on. A large animal has tripped and broken its leg. The priests don't want to help carry the animal to the temple because it's no longer fit to be sacrificed. The man who brought the animal cannot lift it by himself and it's blocking the road. On important holidays it takes hours to reach the temple. Most Jews visit the temple once a year, deliver their animal, and hurry back home. A patient scholar can observe the priests and their sacrifices for an entire day but most Jews would rather remain home and make promises. They find it easier to pay strong attention to something when they have made a promise about it. Someone says: I promise to consider this or this a sacrifice and I will keep it separate from everything else and the next time that I'm in Jerusalem I will bring it to the temple. Or someone says: I promise not to do this or this for one year and to consider this not-doing a sacrifice. The temple is destroyed. The Jews want to continue to make promises. But they can no longer promise to separate something to bring it to the temple later. The promises change. Someone says: I promise to do this or this for you. Or someone says: I promise to think of you when I see a sunset. Someone may not promise that he will not touch his wife for a year. That promise isn't valid. CHAIRMAN: His wife may embrace and hold him until he gives in. RABBI: A promise doesn't count if someone promises something while he's feeling angry or desperate or threatened. The court may release someone from a promise if someone has promised something that's shameful for his parents or for his children or for his wife. If the promise is shameful for himself the promise can be made invalid too. CHAIRMAN: Does it make a difference whether there's a witness present when someone makes an embarrassing promise?

RABBI: Someone says: I promise not to marry this ugly girl. Someone else hears this and makes his wife and daughters spend a day to make the girl beautiful. Then he invites the man who has made the promise. He asks the man whether he would like to drink something. Then he gently claps his hands. The girl enters with a glass of water.

CHAIRMAN: May someone be a witness to a promise if he doesn't hear the promise being made but understands from someone's face that he's making a promise?

RABBI: May someone omit saying the evening prayer and promise to say it the next day twice?

CHAIRMAN: May someone write a divorce letter and promise in the letter to feel love again for someone later?

RABBI: A king asks a woman to marry him and hands her a wedding letter that he's written. The letter says that he will build beautiful wedding night rooms for her and that she will be able to choose the room in which she wants to spend the night and that he will give her the most beautiful jewelry and as many other treasures as she might desire and that he will comb her hair and that he will help her dress and undress. He stays while she hastily reads through the wedding letter's text for the first time. Then he leaves. The wife is left alone. Her friends tell her that she should look for another man. She reads the wedding letter day and night.

CHAIRMAN: My wife and I keep all the letters that we ever wrote to each other. Even the small notes to remind the other to buy bread or milk before the shops close.

RABBI: Who doesn't have time for a wedding? After the wedding you can still think in peace about what type of love you want.

MAIMON: Where is Birobizhan?

RABBI: Somewhere in the east, in Siberia, I believe. It is the land that Stalin gave to the Jews.

MAIMON: The Jews must live there?

RABBI: Only a few Jews are living there. Hardly anyone needs Jews over there. It is a gesture of Stalin, a gesture of his respect for the Jewish people. The situation has also changed since we conquered Jerusalem. Immediately after he had learned the good news Stalin appointed me Chief Rabbi of Birobizhan and Jerusalem.

CHAIRMAN: It's time for a wedding.

RABBI: A man is a slave of two others and one of them sets him free. The patient scholar says that he should continue to serve his remaining master one day and the other day himself. The impatient scholar says: how can he marry? He can neither marry a slave nor a free woman. If a man is a slave of two others and one of them sets him free then the other should set him free too. The patient scholar asks: does that also count for a man who is another one's slave and has bought himself free for the other half? The impatient scholar says: yes. The patient scholar says: and if the slave has bought himself free for one-fourth, or one-twelfth? The impatient scholar says: yes. The patient scholar thinks for a moment and says that he would have gladly been the impatient scholar's slave.

CHAIRMAN: In the middle of the summer the evening sometimes remains warm and heavy. My wife takes a letter that I wrote to her and uses it as a fan.

RABBI: The slave has enough money to immediately buy himself free but he wants to use the money to buy food and drinks for the guests at his wedding party. He invites all of his owners. Do the owners have to set him free immediately when they notice that there are no other guests?

CHAIRMAN: That's how important a wedding is. A funeral procession gives precedence to a wedding procession. Someone studies the law and someone places a wedding invitation on his table; he immediately stops studying and leaves for the place of the wedding celebration. Maimon, Moses' law. Do you want to marry her according to Moses' law?

MAIMON: I don't know Moses' law very well.

CHAIRMAN: That's not an excuse.

RABBI: Do you have a ring? Or maybe a coin?

MAIMON: I'm sorry.

CHAIRMAN: A bottle of perfume? A bouquet of flowers?

RABBI: If he really doesn't have anything he can also give her a hand.

CHAIRMAN: As the promise of a handful?

MAIMON: I have a hand.

CHAIRMAN: You have to take good care of her. She needs to eat and drink every day. At least three meals on a Sabbath. You are not allowed to prevent her from visiting a house where they are mourning someone or a house where they are celebrating.

MAIMON: I will do my best.

CHAIRMAN: You shouldn't ask her to do something that her friends consider unusual. If she is captured during a war you should buy her freedom, even if the price asked for her is much higher than the price that would be paid for her on a slave market. If you have agreed with her not to buy her freedom you should still buy her freedom.

(One of the members of the commission taps on the shoulder of another member of the commission and points to the glass lying on the floor.)

RABBI: Maimon, the glass is not only because of love but

also so as not to forget Jerusalem.

CHAIRMAN: Even now that Jerusalem has been recaptured.

RABBI: Someone is painting a wall and leaves a small part of that wall uncovered because he remembers Jerusalem. A woman is getting dressed. First she chooses a dress and some jewelry from a box in which she keeps her jewelry. She places the necklaces and bracelets and earrings next to the dress on the bed. She puts on the dress and then the jewelry. She leaves one of the jewels on the bed as if she forgot it.

CHAIRMAN: So as not to forget Jerusalem.

RABBI: Someone steps on a glass and breaks it on his wedding day. Before the glass is kicked to pieces the groom and the bride may carefully drink from the glass and write with their tongues the name of the other on a future piece of the glass.

CHAIRMAN: He is a great scholar.

RABBI: If you're wearing a glass shoe or have a foot of glass you may also kick hard against the floor. You may also try to kick the world to pieces.

CHAIRMAN: Isn't that a bit too much?

RABBI: I've read it in a book.

COMMISSION:
Each book has an angel
Studying the book together with the scholar,
Except when the scholar himself becomes the book's angel
When he opens the book.

To want to look at such a man
To find back one's own courage
To really study, not like the angels of books
With each other in heaven.

RABBI: Too much honor.

CHAIRMAN: What is a little bit of honor between a man like you and a man like me?

RABBI: Even Abraham had a study friend when he was an adult. Someone can study so hard that no one can really study together with him? But someone can pose him difficult and important questions and in this way study with him. Abraham studies with the son of a man who heard that he had to build a ship. The man is dead and the son is old. He says something and has immediately forgotten what he said. The only thing that the son remembers easily is what the world looks like when it is fully covered with water. Someone can no longer study that hard but he can still study well and he can explain better what he has studied. Now someone else can really study together with him. Someone notices or is afraid that the moment approaches that the other can really study with him. He asks the other to ask him a final difficult and important question. How does someone recognize a difficult and important question? When dealing with the question seems both frightening and ridiculous?

CHAIRMAN: I would like to study together with you for longer.

RABBI: Two scholars who live in a city and don't discuss the law with each other; one deserves to die, the other to be banished. Whoever causes another to die deserves himself to die but whoever causes death because of a lack of care deserves to be banished. Too harsh a rule? The rule only counts when there are only two scholars living in a city. What is the extent of the city? As far as someone may be expected to travel to attend a funeral? If there are only two scholars in the whole world, and they don't talk with each other about the law, one deserves to die and the other to be banished to a city of refuge.

CHAIRMAN: In the world to come this cannot happen because there will always be more than two scholars there.

RABBI: Someone is inattentive and someone else dies. The inattentive one flees to a city of refuge. The inattentive one remains in that city until the high priest dies. Then he may return and no one may do something to him. If there is no high priest he waits until someone dies in the city from which he fled and the inattentive one would feel ashamed if he wouldn't attend his funeral.

GONCHAROVA: Where is a city of refuge?

RABBI: Why a high priest? A high priest is a beautiful man, maybe the most beautiful man someone has ever seen. He may not be blind or lame. Naturally he may not be deaf-mute. He may not be hunch-backed. His eyes may not be bloodshot the entire day. All priests have strong and undamaged feet.

GONCHAROVA: The priests walk through the temple barefoot?

MAIMON: I don't think they are allowed to wear shoes.

GONCHAROVA: Are you sure? High hats and no shoes?

CHAIRMAN: The temple has been destroyed. There is no high priest.

RABBI: The most beautiful man in the city or village is like the high priest. Maybe the ugliest and unhappiest one too. For someone cannot be angry about inattentiveness on the day that he hears that the ugliest and unhappiest man he knows has died?

CHAIRMAN: The inhabitants of a city fear that they don't pay enough attention. They banish the ugliest man of the city. The inhabitants of a city are afraid that they pay such close attention that they have forgotten to do something and they don't know what. They let the ugliest man get married.

MAIMON: Who marries him?

RABBI: Only after having made the decision to banish the ugliest man the ugliest man is determined. The two or three men who are the ugliest try to ridicule each other in a way that doesn't arouse pity.

CHAIRMAN: When someone is the most beautiful or ugliest man in a village and he's fled because of his own inattentiveness, for whose death should he wait?

RABBI: The high priest has a substitute. One week before the day of atonement the high priest is appointed. The substitute may immediately take the place of the high priest if the high priest can no longer behave like a high priest. A substitute for the high priest's wife is appointed too. Beforehand the high priest asks his wife for forgiveness for his quick remarriage. A high priest has to be married. When the high priest's wife suddenly dies the substitute is ready to marry the high priest. In the days preceding the day of atonement the high priest may not speak to his wife or see her. During those days the high priest is not allowed to sleep. At night he reads the text of the law. If he is no longer able to continue reading one of the younger priests takes the text from his hands and reads it to him. If the high priest seems to be falling asleep the young priests start snapping their fingers as if they want to grab the attention of a waiter.

MAIMON: Which is otherwise not at all allowed?

CHAIRMAN: When a man wants to discuss something with another and he makes that other one?

RABBI: Someone who's been made cannot talk. Idolatry is certainly not allowed. Idolatry is like a prohibited wedding.

CHAIRMAN: Selling or lending a slave to someone who

maybe doesn't know that he has to set the slave free as soon as he begins to speak about a wedding.

RABBI: It doesn't even have to be his own wedding.

CHAIRMAN: It doesn't even have to be an allowed wedding.

RABBI: Someone can marry a slave that he has set free? Someone can marry a slave that he has set free after he has previously enslaved him?

CHAIRMAN: Half a slave or half a question. To whom can we compare him?

RABBI: Someone would like to hear something and laughs about someone who tells it to him.

CHAIRMAN: An idol of a non-Jew is unclean and makes a Jew who touches the idol unclean.

RABBI: The non-Jew can lift the idol's uncleanliness by insulting or damaging the idol.

CHAIRMAN: Immediately afterward the Jew can touch the non-Jew's idol.

RABBI: The non-Jew can break off one of the idol's fingers and kick the idol with his foot. He can leave the idol somewhere like something that he's forgotten or lost and no longer hopes to find back.

CHAIRMAN: The non-Jew can touch the idol and worship with an intention different from the idol. The Jew can touch the idol afterward too? Someone has frightened someone else and thereby caused damage; does he have to compensate the damage? Someone who has frightened someone else by screaming at him or by suddenly emerging from the dark doesn't have to compensate the damage. But he has to compensate the damage if he has touched the other's clothes with a mere finger.

RABBI: If a Jew says about something that it's his idol, is it immediately unclean? The undamaged scholar says that it's only unclean if the Jew has also really worshiped it.

The Jew has to have made at least a bow toward what he claims to worship. But this only counts for something that has been made by someone. For example a piece of wood cut into a shape or a stone that is placed upright. A Jew cannot make a mountain or a living animal unclean by worshiping the mountain or the animal.

GONCHAROVA: Could time become unclean?

RABBI: Can time be worshiped like an idol?

CHAIRMAN: Can something be made from time? Like someone making a chair from wood?

RABBI: Someone separates time from the rest of time; is that making? Someone says: from eight o'clock in the evening until eleven o'clock in the evening I want to study. At ten o'clock in the evening someone else knocks on the door and asks: am I interrupting? If I'm interrupting I'll leave. It's a beautiful evening and I wouldn't mind having a walk for an hour and coming back later. Worshiping the stars is the most complete form of idolatry but it doesn't make the stars unclean. The stars will be fleeing away from us long after the world to come has begun here. An anxious Jew is taking a bath. Not in streaming or falling water but in rainwater that has become still. The rain falls into a bathtub and after it has stopped raining the Jew steps into the filled bath. If there's not enough rain the bath may be filled up with other water. A closable tube may also connect the bath with a deposit of old rainwater. The bath may be filled first with other water and sometimes the tube is opened. The rainwater may touch the other water and make it still. Someone is awake and lies in bed anxiously and sweating and his wife's hand touches him when it's nearly become morning.

CHAIRMAN: A Jew cannot make the water unclean by worshiping it day and night.

MAIMON: Why do Jews consider water so important?

CHAIRMAN: A non-Jew feeling worried or frightened is still advised to take a bath. Or someone gives the non-Jew a glass of water.

RABBI: A Jew touching a dead body has to bathe himself in water. But it is idolatry to act as if the dead body makes unclean or the water removes the uncleanliness. Each part of the law that has no clear other meaning may be explained as a rule against idolatry.

GONCHAROVA: Jews don't consider water important?

RABBI: Someone can become unclean by following the law. For example by caring for a sick person until he dies. Unclean doesn't mean that someone has to remove his uncleanliness before he is allowed to sacrifice.

MAIMON: May I worship Heidegger?

RABBI: When your life is in danger you may worship everything.

CHAIRMAN: Except for wooden or stone statues as if those statues would be able to bring each other to life.

GONCHAROVA: Who has ever seen two wooden statues bring each other to life?

RABBI: Abraham's father has a shop in which he sells statues of idols. He asks his son to help him in the ship. A customer enters the shop and says that he wants to buy an idol. The customer hesitantly points to a statue close to the shop entrance. Abraham picks up a cane. Abraham is a young man yet he has a cane. With the cane he smashes the statue that the customer is pointing at and also the statues next to it. Abraham says: do you want this god? Or this god? The shop doesn't run well and the father decides to sell his son as a slave. Together with Abraham he goes to the market and finds a buyer. When he returns to the shop a client is waiting for him asking for the largest and most expensive idol that is still undamaged. Abraham's father runs to the market and buys his son back.

CHAIRMAN: For a higher price than he sold him for?

RABBI: The buyer has kept Abraham for a short period and has taken care of him.

CHAIRMAN: If a man wants to make a sacrifice and he has no sacrifice and he fabricates a sacrifice, does it count as a sacrifice?

MAIMON: Why count?

CHAIRMAN: Can someone who's been made count?

MAIMON: Someone who's been made a Jew?

RABBI: Making a Jew is different from making an animal or a world.

CHAIRMAN: It is the opposite?

RABBI: Numbers aren't made.

MAIMON: Numbers exist first and only then God?

RABBI: God makes the world. The numbers originate together with the beginning of the making. They are called, not made. In order to make He studies the first text. In the first text words and numbers are so intimately linked that they cannot be distinguished from each other. The first numbers are such that someone who sees an amount of something can immediately say how many there are. Then He separates words and numbers from each other and gives the second text to the Jews. The numbers solidify after they have been separated from the text and become the skeleton of the made world. From the moment that world has been made the numbers desire the text and the text desires the numbers. Abraham is the first one who notices that the text and the numbers have been separated from each other. He notices this while he's still a child but he cannot explain it.

CHAIRMAN: Abraham studies without a study friend while

he is still a child?

RABBI: He studies with the idols in the shop and, at night, with the stars. Someone says that seven things exist before the world is made: the law, a Jew, God's throne, the name of the king of the end of time, reward, punishment, and remorse. If those seven things exist they are hidden in the first text. No one can see them.

MAIMON: The second text is the text of the law?

RABBI: If the law is the second text, the other six consist of numbers who have dressed up awkwardly out of fear for the separation of the text. But the numbers look pitiable, even if they put on a Jew, the throne, the name, reward, punishment, and remorse all on top of each other. I think that no one can say that the law exists before the world is made. The law is called by making, just like the numbers in the world.

CHAIRMAN: What exists before a Jew is made?

RABBI: Someone wants to become a Jew. The Jews surround him and ask him to say a number, a large number, a number so large that the Jews don't know it yet.

CHAIRMAN: And burst out in laughter.

GONCHAROVA: Should I have said a number?

RABBI: No, that's no longer customary.

MAIMON: How can remorse exist before there is something to be remorseful about?

GONCHAROVA: Regret or remorse?

CHAIRMAN: A good difference!

RABBI: An excellent difference. Someone may feel regret before he does something which he will regret? Someone cannot know how he will act yet already have a feeling of regret? He feels an emptiness growing inside and the interior of that emptiness is covered with regret? But remorse in advance doesn't seem possible. Isn't it at most regret in advance if remorse in advance doesn't prevent acting?

CHAIRMAN: An excellent difference.

RABBI: In the world to come maybe someone can feel remorse in advance. Someone cannot decide whether the law has to be explained like this or like this. He imagines that he acts in a way that is prohibited by a particular explanation and he pays attention whether he feels remorse in advance.

CHAIRMAN: Remorse in advance at the beginning and at the end. Someone is not allowed to try to calculate when the end will happen. Is someone allowed to calculate when his wedding will happen? Someone can calculate it as a joke. But not in the presence of someone who could be his bride.

RABBI: In the world to come text and numbers will reunite in the form of music. In the world to come someone sings an explanation of the law and pays attention whether the melody makes him feel remorse. But now is not the moment to speak about remorse.

CHAIRMAN: It is time to get married.

RABBI: You're right. It's time. Maimon, you don't have to worry about your marriage. You don't have to worry about what you're feeling when you want to touch her.

CHAIRMAN: He doesn't have to worry. He may touch her anywhere. The first fathers and mothers touched each other everywhere and were lying in bed laughing. Your parents and your grandparents touched each other. Sometimes I'm overwhelmed myself by the need to touch my wife. In the middle of the day I take an hour off and go home as quickly as possible. Of course the bride doesn't have to worry. It's difficult to explain marriage to an unmarried man.

GONCHAROVA: Shouldn't I have worn a veil? And a white

dress?

RABBI: It's enough to wave your spread-out fingers quickly back and forth in front of your face once. You don't have to do it now. Later is fine too.

CHAIRMAN: The bride's face illuminates the room, even if she's holding both hands in front of her face.

RABBI: Each wedding guest is required to make an effort to make the bride feel happy on her wedding day. This bride is beautiful but when a bride is ugly and dull? The patient big scholar and the impatient big scholar have different opinions. The patient scholar says that the wedding guest has to tell the bride that she is gorgeous and gracious, even if she isn't. The impatient scholar says that lying is still prohibited and that the wedding guest has to try to make the bride happy without saying that she's looking beautiful. In this world the law according to the patient scholar applies but in the world to come the law according to the impatient scholar applies.

CHAIRMAN: The law is applied according to the explanation of the majority of scholars. The majority is following the patient scholar.

COMMISSION MEMBER: If it's about the explanation prescribing or prohibiting an action.

RABBI: If there's no majority of scholars the explanation applies that allows the behavior of the majority. In order not to embarrass the majority. At the end of a Jewish war the temple is destroyed. A scholar suggests that because of the mourning of the temple it is no longer allowed to sleep with a woman. The other scholars tell him: it is wrong to make a decision that the majority cannot support. Which majority? The majority of Jews in the city in which the scholars are assembled? How to determine the behavior of the majority? The scholars come into the city and look around. They try not to show what behavior they are looking at. In order not to change the behavior by looking at it? In order not to embarrass? If it's about the behavior happening in a bathhouse they visit bath-houses. If it's about buying and selling they visit shops. If it's about behavior happening in bedrooms? It is embar-rassing to visit bedroom after bedroom and to count.

CHAIRMAN: This bride is more beautiful than any other woman ever on her wedding day.

COMMISSION MEMBER: This bride makes all wedding dresses superfluous.

CHAIRMAN: The most unprepared witness sees this bride in the way she most prefers to see herself.

COMMISSION MEMBER: This bride may wear all jewels.

RABBI: Like a necklace around her soft neck. The crown is thought and thought leads to wisdom and wisdom to understanding and understanding to pity and pity to fear and fear leads to beauty and beauty to victory and vic-tory to glory and glory to the indispensable that is also called groom and the indispensable leads to the regality that is also called bride and sometimes also Madam Pres-ence. The world to come opens itself at the end of the year when for an entire year each bride that marries in that year feels happy on her wedding day. At the end of that year all brides gather at the entrance of the world to come and stand in two long lines in between which the living who have justified their lives and the dead who have been raised up pass to enter the world to come. The brides laugh and clap their hands and only after the last just one has entered the world to come the brides run behind them like happy little girls.

CHAIRMAN: This bride is as beautiful as the Sabbath.

RABBI: Someone may save a life by doing something that

is prohibited on the Sabbath. Also on a Sabbath the text of the law has to be saved from a burning house. Someone cannot determine from the sun or the stars whether it is a Sabbath. What applies for the Sabbath also applies for the world to come.

CHAIRMAN: A burning house in the world to come?

COMMISSION:
Someone is traveling through a desert
And doesn't know which day it is;
He counts six days from the day
On which he notices that he no longer knows

And on the seventh day he celebrates the Sabbath.
A patient one says this. An impatient one says:
When he notices that he no longer knows
He has to celebrate immediately.

CHAIRMAN: To see this bride any man would want travel an entire life.

GONCHAROVA: I'm so happy that you could be at my wedding.

CHAIRMAN: Her skin shines as if rubbed in moonlight.

RABBI: It's sufficient for the bride and groom to lie in the same bed and the witnesses to stand around it. The bride and groom lie still or move and the witnesses shout and sing.

MAIMON: Whom are the witnesses shouting at?

RABBI: At everyone who wants to listen and the bride and groom may listen along too and become even happier when they hear how they are and what they are for each other. A witness who has an interest in the outcome of a court case is not allowed to testify. This also applies to a witness at a wedding. This seems to exclude a man who would have liked to marry the bride from being a witness. But a witness is also a guest at the wedding and has to praise the bride.

CHAIRMAN: Who wouldn't want to marry this bride?

RABBI: The second point is more important than the first one. Someone who is unable to praise the bride in a way that suggests that he would have liked to marry the bride cannot be a witness. Someone who is seriously ill and thinks that he no longer has enough force to hold the bride in bed.

MAIMON: He cannot be a witness?

CHAIRMAN: He can watch but he cannot act as witness. The court doesn't listen to him. Just like the court doesn't listen to a child, a slave, an imbecile, or deaf-mute. The court doesn't listen to someone who has an interest in what he is a witness of. The court doesn't listen to a family member of someone who has an interest. The court doesn't listen to someone who has violated the law and shows no remorse. The court doesn't listen to someone who doesn't seem to be able to feel ashamed, for example, someone who eats impatiently while walking on the street.

RABBI: If someone cannot be ashamed, how can he be a witness?

CHAIRMAN: How can God be ashamed? And if the Sabbath is the bride and the Jewish people the groom?

COMMISSION:
She's squatting on the ground
On an unfolded prayer scarf.
A voice calls softly,
She gets up, wraps herself in the scarf.

The groom watches from afar,
Thinks while he watches

How to undress her naked,
As if fled from her lovers.

RABBI: May God be a witness in the world to come?
CHAIRMAN: I asked you. May someone refrain from being a witness while he could have been a witness?
RABBI: A child says: I can say that my father and mother and all my brothers and sisters are dead and everyone who hears it will pity me. This is the reason that a child may not be a witness? A witness cannot withdraw from the obligation to be a witness like a child saying that he's had enough of seeing you: why aren't you dead already?
CHAIRMAN: He's not allowed?
RABBI: He's not but the court cannot force him to compensate the damage he has caused by not testifying. This also holds when the witness is the only witness of something of which there should be two witnesses. It smells like a failed sacrifice but that's none of our business; we don't have time.
CHAIRMAN: I asked you.
RABBI: A witness who has made everything? Who has made humans? Who has made women? Who causes bride and groom to be made happy like Jerusalem makes Him happy? Who causes husband and wife to be happy as if they were the first man and woman in the garden? Who has made happiness, bride and groom, pleasure, love, friendship, and peace? Who causes no one to be able to be ashamed any longer and no one to be able to be a witness any longer; everyone is bride or groom and the streets of Jerusalem are full of happy shouting from beds?
CHAIRMAN: Someone is not allowed to be a witness and wants to be a witness.
RABBI: He may be a witness if he feels remorse for that

which caused him no longer to be allowed to be a witness. He doesn't have to say aloud that he feels remorse. He has to say it aloud to receive forgiveness but not in order to feel remorse. Someone has insulted someone else. He asks the other to forgive him. If the other doesn't forgive him he should have three friends asking for forgiveness in his name. If the other still isn't prepared to forgive him he should have three other friends ask for it, and then yet three other friends. Someone has made someone else sad. How can he ask for forgiveness? By asking forgiveness for everything he has done wrong, carelessly or carefully? By remembering each separate instance he did something wrong and separately asking for forgiveness? May he count the separate instances if he remembers them one by one?

CHAIRMAN: This bride is as beautiful as the Sabbath.

RABBI: Does God know it is the Sabbath? He asks someone not to do something and that someone still does it. Then it becomes night. That's how the Sabbath feels to God.

CHAIRMAN: What else can we do?

RABBI: The chairs?

CHAIRMAN: Of course, the chairs! Just a moment!

(The commission runs away and nearly immediately returns with two heavy armchairs which it places in front of Maimon and Goncharova. Goncharova sits down in one of the chairs.)

MAIMON: Should I sit down in the chair?

RABBI: The groom is the king.

MAIMON: I'm not sure whether that's such a good idea.

RABBI: When the king is dancing his feet don't have to touch the floor. It's an old habit. Do me that favor.

MAIMON: I cannot dance.

RABBI: All the more reason to sit down in the chair. You're being danced.

MAIMON: There's no music?

RABBI: You want music?

MAIMON: To dance?

RABBI: Now you want music and soon you want music when you're touching your wife and then music when you're watching your wife sleeping. Later you won't be able to do that without music?

(Maimon sits down in the chair. The members of the commission divide themselves in two groups and try to hoist the chairs with Maimon and Goncharova onto their shoulders, which doesn't work. They put the chairs down.)

RABBI: Couldn't you find lighter chairs? Try to hold the bride and groom at least a bit above the floor.

(With difficulty they raise the chairs a bit above the floor.)

RABBI: Dancing won't work. Carry them away.

berlin

MRS. HEIDEGGER: Martin, why don't you sing anymore? As a child you used to have a beautiful voice.

HEIDEGGER: I could never really sing.

MRS. HEIDEGGER: As I child you could sing.

HEIDEGGER: Mother, I could never sing.

MRS. HEIDEGGER: You used to speak so beautifully.

HEIDEGGER: I still speak with you.

MRS. HEIDEGGER: You call that speaking? Why don't you read a bit to me from the remembering book.

HEIDEGGER: That book makes me sick.

(Heidegger walks up to a closed cupboard. Takes out a small but thick book.)

MRS. HEIDEGGER: Just begin somewhere in the middle.

HEIDEGGER: Greim, Jakob, died 1924, heart attack, Bleichröderstrasse 25a; Greinstetter, Markus, died 1933, old age, Nymphenburgerstrasse 166; Greinstetter, Amalia, died 1939, old age, Nymphenburgerstrasse 166; Grosz, Anna Frederika, died 1913, lung disease, Sanatorium Franszenbad; Grueber, Nikolaus, died 1930, fall from window, Tauenzienstrasse 6.

MRS. HEIDEGGER: Do you remember Grueber? The old baker. I often used to go to his shop. His son still runs the shop but the bread is not as good. Now when I'm home I usually buy it at Lewetzov. Just continue.

HEIDEGGER: Grüssbach, Eleanore, died 1912, old age, Maximilianstrasse 137; Grüssbach, Peter, died 1917, bullet in the head, field hospital Montreuil; Grüssbach, Max, died 1917, old age, Bleichröderstrasse 137; Grüssbach, Paul Joachim, died 1917, sudden blood loss, Ostend; Grüssbach, Sebastian Alexander, died 1917, wound poisoning, Ostend; Grüssbach, Anton, died 1937, torn apart by wild animal, Bleichröderstrasse 137; Grüssbach, Andrea, died 1940, tiredness, Bleichröderstrasse 137; Grüssbach, Elizabeth, died 1940, lung disease, Bleichröderstrasse 137.

MRS. HEIDEGGER: That is the villa at the end of the Bleichröderstrasse. As a child you were sometimes allowed to play with the other children in their garden. The Grüssbachs used to have a pond and a swing. Max Grüssbach was a rich and honest man. He lived with his wife and his children in that large house.

HEIDEGGER: May I stop?

MRS. HEIDEGGER: Just two or three more. For my pleasure.

HEIDEGGER: Günther, Hendrik. There were really a lot of Günthers.

MRS. HEIDEGGER: There are still many Günthers. They marry young and live long. Still we never got along well. In shops they often tried to skip the line. Just do the first three ones. To make your mother happy.

HEIDEGGER: Günther, Hendrik, died 1912, lung disease and heart attack.

MRS. HEIDEGGER: As if one cause of death were not enough.

HEIDEGGER: Lung disease and heart attack, southern Germany, exact location unknown.

MRS. HEIDEGGER: He needed the whole of southern Germany.

HEIDEGGER: Günther, Arnold, died 1912, old age, Lessingstrasse 11, Günther, Anna Magdalena, died 1915, old age, Lessingstrasse 11.

(Mrs. Heidegger looks over Heidegger's shoulder at the page he's reading. She touches his head. Heidegger and Mrs. Heidegger leave the room.)

(Maimon and Goncharova enter, each holding a small suitcase. Goncharova opens her suitcase, looks inside and closes it again. Both sit down on the floor.)

GONCHAROVA: Would we be allowed to lie down here?

MAIMON: I think it's an office. If someone comes to work here they'll chase us out.

GONCHAROVA: Would we be allowed to sleep here?

MAIMON: If someone comes in I will try not to get frightened. If we're both asleep we can perhaps be offended when someone wakes us up.

GONCHAROVA: The rabbi has told me that dreams should not be taken too seriously. That worrying about a terrible dream removes the terror and dissolves the dream just like happiness about a pleasing dream does. Do you talk aloud when you're dreaming?

MAIMON: The rabbi must have been a good teacher.

GONCHAROVA: A very good teacher. The best I ever had, except maybe Meyerhold.

MAIMON: I've seen Meyerhold only once, from far away. He directed a show by graduating students, now two years ago. Did you play in that show?

GONCHAROVA: I took part in the show of the year before that. That was my graduation year. It was a Jewish play.

MAIMON: Your own?

GONCHAROVA: A normal play but we all wore Jewish masks.

MAIMON: A few of my classmates wanted to act like that already in the first year.

GONCHAROVA: It's allowed in the second year. That's also when you are not allowed to speak the shortest sentence before you have found each word and each gesture in a memory.

MAIMON: There must have been a lot of crying.

GONCHAROVA: There was an awful lot of crying. And laughing and everything. When someone fully plays in that way the word "truth" appears on his forehead.

MAIMON: In luminous letters? An invitation to a kiss on the forehead?

GONCHAROVA: Sometimes. In the third year we were no longer allowed to work like that. But then we were again allowed to put on masks. We were allowed to make them ourselves but if it didn't work we could also borrow one from his supply. Only the masks of Meyerhold's own teacher were off limits. Meyerhold's teacher spent his evenings acting and teaching. During the day he was the director of a small factory which produced the masks. The laborers wore uniforms resembling the evening attire of a rich man going out for dinner in a restaurant. A few of those uniforms were hanging in the same wardrobe that Meyerhold used for his collection of military uniforms.

MAIMON: The only time I saw him he was wearing normal clothes.

GONCHAROVA: On the first day of the theater ban Stalin appointed Meyerhold as honorary field marshal. Early in the morning a postman came at his door and handed him a flat cartboard box. The box contained a folded-up field marshal's uniform.

MAIMON: In my first year I took puppetry as an elective. There were only two students in the puppetry class. The other one was expelled from the school by the end of the first year, just like me. According to the teacher you can always earn money with puppetry, even if theater doesn't work out. The other student found a job at an academy for lower civil servants and shop assistants. He played different types of customers standing in line before a counter. That's how the civil servant or shop assistant learns how to deal with someone who spits on the ground or pushes other people away or continues to scream at him.

GONCHAROVA: I know someone who used to do that type of work but after the theater ban he also went to do something else.

MAIMON: I was worried that from that moment puppetry would also no longer be allowed. I went to the police headquarters to ask whether it was allowed or not. I asked the first officer I saw. He pointed me to a chair in the hallway. I waited for an hour and then another officer came and asked me to come with him. He walked in front of me through long hallways. Eventually he opened a door and told me to go in. A man wearing a long coat and a hat was sitting in a small and quiet office. The man told me to return the next morning. The next morning I was immediately sent to a much larger room in which the chief of police was sitting. His uniform was covered with decorations. He got up and two or three decorations jumped from his chest. He shook my hand and told me roaring with laughter that they had made an exception for me. He said: have a seat. There was no other chair in the room than the one he was sitting on. I acted as if I carefully looked around trying to find an empty chair. He started laughing again. His face got red. He laughed so loudly that other officers came to check what was going on. Finally he was completely out of breath and asked for a glass of water. He gulped down the glass and said: your puppetry doesn't fall under the theater ban. Don't you ever show up here again.

GONCHAROVA: Puppet shows can be very moving.

MAIMON: Not my puppet shows. I performed for children, mostly not older than six, seven. The children tried to touch my puppets or grab them. I always had to pay attention that they didn't pull the puppets off my hands. They also kicked the stage with their shoes.

GONCHAROVA: Meyerhold once did a puppet show for me. Without a stage. Only with two socks on his hands. One of his and one of mine. I was still in bed.

MAIMON: His bed?

GONCHAROVA: No, my bed. At that time I had a really good bed. Only the room was always cold. I was lying under the blankets and he stood naked in front of the bed with the socks on his hands.

MAIMON: Did he often sleep at your place?

GONCHAROVA: No. Two or three times. Of course he is also at least three times my age. After he finished with the socks he began to dance around naked in the room. It wasn't really dancing; he jumped back and forth and did a somersault. He made a forced happy face. I asked what kind of music he was hearing in his head. He said: no music. The following day the old woman who lives in the room underneath my room stood in front of my door. She complained at length about the noise. I said that I had practiced dance moves. She shook her head. I said that it wouldn't happen again. In any case I had already decided no longer to allow Meyerhold to sleep over at my place.

MAIMON: Did you ever do puppetry yourself?

GONCHAROVA: Meyerhold said that his teacher distinguished between three types of actors. The first one is the plumber-carpenter-actor whose costume is filled with tools. When he's nervous he begins to walk back and forth and his hands begin to shake when he opens a letter or when he fills a glass. When he's sad he holds back his tears. When he dies he reaches for his heart. When he says "large" he makes a large gesture. The second type is the actor-actor who thoroughly studies his role and finds for each feeling a truthful form which he then performs on stage. The third type is the living actor who feels on stage the feeling that he portrays. A puppet in puppetry is the purest plumber-carpenter but he has the excuse that he's just a puppet. Meyerhold removes this excuse. He says that he wants to erase the difference between the three types of actors. A puppet has to be like a living actor while a real actor has to learn how to act like a puppet which has finally managed to become a living actor. Before we begin rehearsing a piece we first have to read the piece together. We sit at a large table and read aloud. The roles have not yet been distributed. We take turns at reading a page. The next one continues where the page ends, sometimes halfway through a sentence. To prepare for the collective reading we play with puppets at home and have the puppets take turns at reading a page too. Puppetry is good exercise.

MAIMON: Especially with socks.

GONCHAROVA: The simpler the puppet the more you learn from it, he said.

MAIMON: Naked with a sock on each hand and the audience in bed.

GONCHAROVA: A nice and large bed.

MAIMON: Where to watch and listen better than in your own bed?

GONCHAROVA: Did you have nice puppets?

MAIMON: If Meyerhold thought puppetry was so important, why didn't he give it as an elective? I was taught by an old lady who made her puppets from her own worn-out clothes, in which she took a lot of pride. Meyerhold must have been too busy. Or was the old lady Meyerhold's mother?

GONCHAROVA: His mother died in her sleep a long time ago.

(Benjamin enters. Maimon and Goncharova get up in a hurry.)

GONCHAROVA: Is this your room? We were just looking for a place to sleep in this building. We are foreigners.

BENJAMIN: Foreigners from where?

GONCHAROVA: Russia. We've fled.

BENJAMIN: Do you hope that someone asks you to be guests? Rightful guests receive kisses. At arrival and departure.

MAIMON: We are refugees.

BENJAMIN: Wanderers?

MAIMON: Refugees.

BENJAMIN: Fleeing from what?

MAIMON: Suppression.

BENJAMIN: Suppression by what?

MAIMON: Suppression of the theater.

BENJAMIN: You've fled in the wrong direction. We're actually just working on putting a definitive end to the theater. Are you sure you're not tourists?

GONCHAROVA: That is a joke?

BENJAMIN: It's very serious. I take it very seriously. It's about the old goddesses.

GONCHAROVA: In Russia we've never heard about them.

BENJAMIN: About the old goddesses? The old goddesses are anger, shame, love, fear, mourning, revenge, and five or six others. Before, a theater used to be a temple of the goddesses.

MAIMON: We thought that the situation in Berlin was different. That theater was still being made here.

BENJAMIN: The Jews are against theater and the Jews have won, as usual.

MAIMON: There are still theaters in Berlin, right?

BENJAMIN: Of course there are still theaters in Berlin. Half of all the income of the theaters goes to homes for people who can no longer take care of themselves: orphanages, retirement homes, and homes for the weak of mind. Someone who cannot take care of himself may also visit the theater for half-price. By the way, can I offer you a drink?

(Benjamin gestures in the direction of two chairs standing against the wall.)

BENJAMIN: Put the chairs next to the desk and sit down. Are you foreigners perhaps? What kind of theater did you play in Russia?

MAIMON: Puppetry. After a year they expelled me from the theater academy.

GONCHAROVA: I was taught by Meyerhold.

BENJAMIN: Theater or film?

GONCHAROVA: Theater and film. Meyerhold says that film is a good exercise for theater. The face and the body appear larger on the projection screen than in reality and that's why feelings can be expressed more carefully.

BENJAMIN: Meyerhold knows what he's talking about. A one-kilometer-wide projection screen. A small vibration of a lip or an eyebrow is enough for half a dozen scenes. Can I offer you something?

(Benjamin takes a bottle of wine and a silver plate with three small wine glass from a drawer. He fills the glasses and serves them. He sits down on the desk, with his feet on a chair. Maimon and Goncharova are sitting on two chairs in front of the desk.)

BENJAMIN: To whom shall we drink?

MAIMON: I've always been an admirer of Heidegger.

BENJAMIN: To Heidegger! When I met him for the first time he was like a hidden king. The winning lottery ticket. You can empty your glasses in one go. There is no ocean in them. Do you first want to say a blessing over the wine? Shall I do it?

GONCHAROVA: When did you first speak with him?

BENJAMIN: I cannot remember precisely. It must have been more than twenty years ago. The first time I saw him I probably didn't even speak with him. Maybe we were introduced by a hostess or host. Eventually I walked up to him and told him that there was something in one of his texts that I didn't understand very well. I asked him whether we could make an appointment to talk about it. He received me in his office at the university. He asked where I had studied, what I thought about my professors, whether I liked long walks. After that I visited him more often, at the university but also at his home. I didn't want to visit him unexpectedly and disturb him during his work. So we agreed that he would put a large plant on the windowsill when he could be disturbed. When he didn't want to be disturbed the plant would remain on the floor. On the other side of the street there was a café and that's where I would often wait.

MAIMON: I have read Heidegger's dinner table conversations three times over. I have used parts of them as text for a puppet show.

BENJAMIN: Initially we talked for hours with neither of us becoming tired. We talked until one of us noticed that the night had passed and that it was getting light again. When I would return to my room after such a conversation I couldn't fall asleep. I often went back outside to walk around the city without noticing where I was going. Sometimes I ended up in the café across from his house where I would drink a cup of coffee and read the newspapers. Since he became chancellor we've no longer had such conversations. In fact they had already ended before he became chancellor. At first he still spoke with the visitors who stayed after dinner. Then he also stopped speaking at the table. Nowadays he doesn't speak with anyone except his mother, for the past ten years already.

GONCHAROVA: Not even with you?

BENJAMIN: I'll get Martin. Something else I can do for you?

MAIMON: Are you sure about the theater?

BENJAMIN: That it's dead?

MAIMON: Does Heidegger think so too?

BENJAMIN: I no longer know what Heidegger is thinking. I'll get him for you. First there are only the old goddesses. Then the royal gods and goddesses arrive. The royal gods are always worried about the old goddesses. They are trying to take away the old goddesses' power or act as if they already have done so. There are plays about that. Humans slaughter other humans whom they mistake for animals and sometimes animals they mistake for humans. Sometimes they think that the royal gods and goddesses want to be their allies against the old goddesses but they are always betrayed and abandoned too early. There are also old plays in which people think that they have an alliance with a royal god but as soon as a single old goddess appears they abandon the royal god. Sometimes the royal gods take revenge on them, at other times the old goddesses. They eat their children and their children eat them. Sometimes there is shouting because somebody notices that he has been mistaken.

MAIMON: The Jews think so?

BENJAMIN: Aren't you Jews? What kind of Jews are you, old ones or new ones?

GONCHAROVA: I'm new.

BENJAMIN: God, the king of the old Jews, is against theater. Someone remembers that a royal god or goddess has done something to him. A Jew who remembers this may in no case reenact this, he may however recount it so slowly that someone else can write it down word by word. Maybe children or weakminded people aren't able to recount like that and are allowed to reenact it. Naturally deaf-mutes are also allowed to reenact it. Once our best architects proposed to build an enormous temple for the old goddesses, in the middle of Berlin, so big that half of Berlin would have to be destroyed. What was supposed to happen in that temple? The old Jews like to talk about slaughtering. May an animal be sedated before the slaughtering begins? An animal that's already dead may not be slaughtered. What if an animal has been so lightly sedated that it could come round and continue its life unaffected if it hadn't been slaughtered? When the animal is not sedated the butchers do their best to calm it down. The animals are left at least a full hour in the waiting room after they've been brought to the slaughterhouse. There they can come to their senses. Some people suggest to paint the walls of the waiting room green. An animal flees from the butcher and runs to a temple where it clings to the altar.

GONCHAROVA: I've never had to learn the laws of slaughtering.

MAIMON: Maybe there was no time for it.

BENJAMIN: When small children begin to study the law they begin with the temple and the sacrifices and the slaughtering.

MAIMON: Women are not allowed to slaughter?

BENJAMIN: A deaf-mute may not slaughter. But a blind man may slaughter if he knows how to slaughter. When someone slaughters at night, in the dark, and he slaughters in the right way, then the slaughtering is legitimate.

GONCHAROVA: And if there are no more men?

BENJAMIN: Then surely women may slaughter. Even if there is no more time. Obligations to do something linked to specific times do not apply to women. For example the morning prayer. There are exceptions. An exception? Women celebrate the holidays which occur at specific times in the year? Or is the obligation not meant for her but for the nearest man? The first man who needs to make time for her when she wants to say she's happy? And when there's no man nearby? When she is an orphan and unmarried and lives in her own house? When all men are dead and she's the only one left behind? She's still not obliged to celebrate the holiday? Time is something very sensitive between Jews and their wives. The men don't want to hear the women sing and don't want to see them dance because of the counting of time. That's one of the many good reasons to dislike Jews.

MAIMON: Women may not sing?

GONCHAROVA: A man may not listen. The voice of a singing woman can confuse him.

BENJAMIN: But he may listen to several women who are singing simultaneously when their voices mingle in such a way that the listener cannot follow single one in particular.

MAIMON: But women may listen to a singing man?

GONCHAROVA: The rabbi says: enjoy it.

BENJAMIN: And when women and men are singing simultaneously? May a man listen to a laughing woman? How does Abraham invent the morning prayer? It's a terrible enterprise to connect a prayer to a certain moment of the day. He wakes up and walks outside, quietly, so as not to wake up the animals. He's standing outside as if he's standing in the middle of a long line of waiting people.

MAIMON: Is Hitler the best architect?

BENJAMIN: Hitler shows me a proposal for an opera theater. The stage floats on water and is surrounded by high mountains. The audience stands along the shores of the lake. The musicians sit in a large watertight barge between the shore and the stage. The walls of the barge stick out just above the water. What is the question?

GONCHAROVA: And when there's a thunderstorm?

BENJAMIN: The stage moves along with the waves. Sometimes the top of a wave may spill onto the musicians.

GONCHAROVA: Hitler is a good architect?

BENJAMIN: Of course. After he resigned I still often talked with him about temples. The last thing he proposed to me was a wall right across Berlin. From the north to the southernmost point where the city ends and one suddenly sees only green fields. The wall would be like a fully unfolded temple. I say that it is a great proposal but I don't know whether the city is ready for it. Hitler proposed to build the wall within one night and to destroy it again in the same night.

MAIMON: I have always wondered how a man like Hitler could so suddenly decide to resign.

BENJAMIN: On a beautiful day.

MAIMON: In the middle of the summer?

BENJAMIN: Earlier. It's early April. Martin lives in a rented villa in a suburb. I pick him up in a taxi. Martin comes outside, says that he has forgotten something and runs back inside. I'm standing next to the taxi and for the first time that year I'm seeing trees in blossom. Martin comes outside and I point out the trees to him. Martin says that he already noticed them a few days ago.

GONCHAROVA: What did Heidegger forget?

MAIMON: You were present at Hitler's resignation?

BENJAMIN: In this very room. The desk and the chairs are new. After his resignation Hitler would like to take his furniture to his new house. Naturally Martin agrees. It's a sunny day. Martin is very nervous and complains about the heat. Martin is wearing his best dark blue suit, not his professorial robe. Hitler is wearing his uniform. We enter the room and Hitler gets up and embraces Martin. Martin is not very good at embracing. Hitler shakes his hand. Hitler's cap is on the desk. The cap has a metal lining. Hitler has strong neck muscles. Hitler says: a man is unclean. He takes a bath. Does he make the bath water unclean? I say: a man is unclean. He steps into a river. A little further down a man steps into the river; does he become unclean? Hitler nods. I say: a man is standing in music. Another man hears the music but also sees the first man moving to the beat of the music in such a way that he is certain that the music would excite different feelings in him if he wouldn't have to see the first man. Hitler says: a man is clean, listens to music, is suddenly touched and he doesn't know by what. The conversation ends like you know it ends. Hitler picks up his cap from the desk and puts it on Martin's head.

GONCHAROVA: It must have been a solemn moment.

BENJAMIN: What to compare it with? A procession and the statue of a god carried in front. The carriers of the statue notice that they've gotten lost or that they have forgotten where to carry the statue to. They stop and put down the god's statue. The others give them a puzzled look. What can they do so that everyone is able to return home before dark? First music then dance?

GONCHAROVA: Is Heidegger's head the same size as Hitler's head?

BENJAMIN: A statue of the royal god of theater sits between the audience on the first row. One day the god's statue has disappeared. On the side of the road toward the theater they find a foot and a bit further down an arm without a hand. Some say that they can recognize the foot and the arm as belonging to the god of theater. That day lots are drawn among the visitors to the theater to choose who is dressed up as the god of theater. He gets his entrance fee back and he's allowed to sit in the spot normally occupied by the statue. A jug of wine and a cup are placed beside him. He fills the cup and takes a small sip. Shortly after the play has begun he accidentally knocks over the still nearly full cup. The wine spills onto the clothes of the spectators in front of him but they don't complain. They pick up the cup and place it next to the jug and encourage him to drink more. That evening he comes home and cannot fall asleep. His wife asks him what happened during the day. He tells her about the play that he's seen. In a walled city a dead person may be carried around for as long as the carriers want to but once he has left the city he may no longer be brought back. Someone who has touched the dead person and who has not yet taken a bath may not come near the temple. Women may not go further than the first inner wall. Common Jews may come in through the entrance gate of that inner wall but they may not go through the next entrance gate if they are too sick to stand upright. Are you students of Meyerhold?

GONCHAROVA: I took his classes.

MAIMON: I didn't take his classes. I attended the school though.

GONCHAROVA: Meyerhold once told me that he would like all spectators to wear Jewish masks.

BENJAMIN: Theater sickens him as much as it does me. Before the destruction of the temple the scholars reenact in their own homes what the priests do in the temple. When they are children they like to go to the temple to watch the priests and pet the sacrificial animals. Later they invite friends to their homes to eat together as if they were priests eating the remainders of the sacrificial animal after the sacrifice. During and after the dinner they talk with each other about the priests and the temple. They try to think how they would behave if they were priests and the unexpected would happen. But the scholars continue to visit the temple on holidays or whenever there is another occasion. The scholar gives the sacrificial animal to a priest and allows the priest to go on, even if he thinks that he's doing it in the wrong way or at the wrong moment of the day. For the scholar visiting the temple is like a dream. It's strange, sometimes terrible, but he knows he cannot stop it. As he is watching he changes in a direction opposite to the movements he makes and the words he shouts or whispers. Long before the temple is destroyed the priests have stopped worrying about their own sloppiness and clumsiness. A high priest dies and it takes days before anyone notices. Jerusalem is surrounded by a large army of non-Jews. A scholar orders a coffin and lies down in it. His students take the coffin on their shoulders and carry it through the city streets. They shout: make way for a funeral procession. When they arrive at a gate in the city wall they tell the gatekeepers: in order not to make the city more unclean we want to bury our teacher's dead body outside the city. The gatekeepers allow the procession to pass. When the gatekeepers can no longer see them the students put down the coffin. The scholar pushes away the lid and steps out of the coffin. The open coffin is left on the side of the road. Then the city is stormed and destroyed. The temple is destroyed and burnt down. All inhabitants are killed or enslaved. The price of a slave drops more than half on the slave markets in other cities. A new slave no longer has anyone to buy back his freedom or, when he does, that someone tells him that he doesn't have enough money, even though the price is low. The escaped scholar settles together with his students in a small city. There are also other scholars who have fled to a safe place in time or who, being slaves, later walk away from their owner without being pursued. These scholars visit him and some stay to live in the city. The scholars speak with each other about the priests and the temple. How many steps does the priest take with the knife in his hand? In which direction does the blood of the sacrificial animal fall? What does a priest say to another priest at sunset? Sometimes a few scholars take a long walk to the mountain where the temple used to be and where the debris of the collapsed and burnt-down temple is still lying around. Like someone looking for a place that he dreamt about. Later these walks are no longer allowed.

(Benjamin leaves the room. Goncharova sits down on Maimon's lap.)

GONCHAROVA: He talks so much.

MAIMON: Didn't we know that already? So far everything is going well. He trusts us too, I think.

GONCHAROVA: He doesn't make me laugh.

MAIMON: He doesn't make anyone laugh. Didn't they tell us that? What does a Jewish mask look like?

GONCHAROVA: Meyerhold tried to make acting so difficult that the actor needed all his force to be able to stand still on the stage. One time he weighed down all the costumes with metal beads sewn into the inside. The dress I'm wearing weighs more than fifty kilos. Some costumes are first lent for a week to beggars. When we get the costumes back we're not allowed to wash them. He also builds a stage on an incline so that the actors constantly have to hold on to each other or the nailed-down furniture in order not to fall. Try that when you also have to wear a Jewish mask.

MAIMON: Does a Jewish mask look like my face?

GONCHAROVA: I haven't seen a Jewish mask that looked like your face. The best masks also constantly look different depending on the light.

(Heidegger enters the room.)

MAIMON: That's Heidegger.

GONCHAROVA: Hello Mr. Heidegger.

MAIMON: He doesn't talk. Didn't Benjamin just tell us?

GONCHAROVA: That doesn't mean you can't greet him.

MAIMOM: Mr. Heidegger, I am a great admirer.

GONCHAROVA: I hope we're not disturbing you.

MAIMON: Do you know what to say when you see a ruling king for the first time?

GONCHAROVA: Two different blessings, one because of meeting a king and one because of seeing something for the first time. But I don't know them by heart.

(Heidegger walks up to them. He takes Goncharova's hand and shakes it. Followed by Maimon's hand. Then he sits down on the chair where Goncharova was sitting before.)

MAIMON: Hello Mr. Heidegger.

GONCHAROVA: You don't have to act as if he's old and weird.

MAIMON: How would I do that? He doesn't answer.

GONCHAROVA: Mr. Heidegger, we are happy to be here and to meet you.

MAIMON: We are happy to be allowed to be guests here.

GONCHAROVA: Mr. Heidegger, we hope that you will never be embarrassed in this world or in the one to come.

(Heidegger gets up from the chair and sits down on the desk, at the spot where Benjamin had been sit. He gestures to the wine and refills their glasses. The glass left by Benjamin, too.)

GONCHAROVA: Thank you, Mr. Heidegger.

MAIMON: Thank you, Mr. Heidegger.

GONCHAROVA: Thank you, Mr. Heidegger.

MAIMON: Thank you, Mr. Heidegger.

GONCHAROVA: You don't have to raise your voice. He isn't deaf.

MAIMON: I didn't raise my voice. Mr. Heidegger, may we drink to your health?
GONCHAROVA: We already drank to Heidegger.
MAIMON: But he wasn't present then.

(Heidegger empties Benjamin's glass.)

GONCHAROVA: Thank you, Mr. Heidegger.

(Benjamin reenters the room. Goncharova gets up. Maimon gets up. Heidegger remains seated.)

BENJAMIN: I cannot find him and here he is already. Martin, these are Solomon Maimon and Natalia Goncharova. They're from Moscow that's burning. Because it's nearly always night there.
MAIMON: Mr. Heidegger.
BENJAMIN: He doesn't want to speak. Didn't I tell you? He keeps silent. I've already proposed to him once that he acquire a guide dog for the silent. To make life easier for all of us. Don't blame me that he no longer talks. He stopped by himself. Before he could hardly stop speaking.
MAIMON: The years of the dinner table conversations.
BENJAMIN: Not years but weeks, maybe four or five months. He talked so much that in hindsight it seemed years. I'm not very good at sitting in a chair and listening for long. My stomach begins to bother me, especially when I have to eat and listen at the same time. First he invites powerful people, mayors and generals and who knows who else. He has to shout the same question three times over before they briefly answer. Later the guests comprise mainly his mother, a few childhood friends, and drivers and secretaries. The secretaries of course attend

79

from the beginning because they write down the text of the conversations. Then he says that he no longer wants to speak during dinner. He says that he wants to live like a farmer. He only wants to reveal his thoughts or decisions in the form of poems. The poems become longer and longer and he starts using words that he invented himself or that he uses in a different manner than the majority. I say: isn't the poet the one who tries to separate something out of language as it is used inattentively that can be sacrificed as a guilt sacrifice because of the inattentiveness? I have to admit that I thought five minutes about this sentence before I said it. Then I asked him why he didn't rather try to write down his text in the form of a dialogue. Often he doesn't manage to finish the poem in time. Of course it's often not possible to keep postponing an important announcement. I ask: did you finish already? Today it really should be finished. They're waiting for it. Then he gives up and a civil servant is allowed to write the text in a great hurry. Sometimes he manages to finish the poem in time though. The declaration of war against Stalin is one of his better poems.

GONCHAROVA: He doesn't look like a farmer.

BENJAMIN: No? Like a man from the countryside who has lost his country? Does he look like a deaf-mute? A deaf-mute is like a child or someone who is weak of mind. Someone is inattentive when he sends a child or a deaf-mute on an errand to bring something to someone else or to deliver a letter. Why do special rules apply to a deaf-mute? Because a deaf-mute makes you think of an idol? The rules for deaf-mutes do not apply to every deaf-mute. They don't apply to one who can gesture and can understand gestures and if he can move and be moved by gestures. Does gesturing only mean speaking in sign language? If the deaf-mute can dance between others who dance and walk between others who walk and stand still between others who stand still and watch between others who watch, does he count as a deaf-mute?

GONCHAROVA: He is still able to speak, right?

BENJAMIN: Ask him to deliver a letter. The show is about to begin. I hope you want to take part.

GONCHAROVA: Do we have to take part in a show?

MAIMON: We didn't prepare ourselves.

BENJAMIN: It isn't necessary to be prepared now. Not for this. This show is an episode of the revenge of the old goddesses.

GONCHAROVA: But we're Jews.

BENJAMIN: Ok, you're Jews. What kind of Jews? A priest makes a sacrifice but he is supposed to make another sacrifice. A peace sacrifice instead of a guilt sacrifice. Is it legitimate when a peace sacrifice is made like a guilt sacrifice? A chicken lays an egg while the chicken is on the verge of the Sabbath. What is the intention of the chicken's owner? How much intention does the chicken's owner have? As much as is necessary to buy or sell the chicken or to promise the chicken to someone. This intention has been invented by the old Jews who watch the temple burn. The new old Jews first want to bring the interpretation of the law in agreement with the changes in the majority's customs, then also with the expected changes in the customs, and then they begin to invent new customs that are in agreement with their feelings. New old Jews see a group of old goddesses standing somewhere on a street corner and think that if one of those ladies had a husband she could become the best possible housewife. The chosen old goddess transforms into a woman who gets up when it's still night and with her own hands prepares food for the family. It's still night and the old goddess sits at the kitchen table spinning the egg on the table like a top to see whether it's fresh. When the old Jews want to help the new old Jews they begin a conversation with them about the chicken. Because I also want to help I talk about the chicken's feelings in the chicken's head. Today you are the chicken. The chicken doesn't need to prepare itself.

MAIMON: Jewish chicken?

BENJAMIN: No matter what kind of chicken. Maybe the show started with an old custom concerning the chicken. Transfer all mistakes from an entire year to the chicken, grab one of the chicken's legs and swing it around three times.

GONCHAROVA: How does the chicken agree to the transfer?

MAIMON: Above the head?

BENJAMIN: Where else? But the chicken doesn't really need to prepare itself. Today's show is a limited version of a larger show. This show already approximates that larger show when the participants are transported somewhere and remain there for a longer period. Small wooden houses, just a bedroom with a roof, on the river shore. Every day the participants get up, eat breakfast, and immediately start discussing the chicken's feelings of that day. At the end of the day they get an abundant supper, drinks at the bar, dancing, walks lit by moonlight or burning torches. All-inclusive exile. For one week or two weeks.

MAIMON: Each day another chicken?

BENJAMIN: What is an indispensable part of a good supper? A king has a son and the son thinks he's a chicken. He doesn't sit down on a chair but crawls under a table and begins to cackle and to move his arms like wings. The king doesn't know what to do. One by one the ministers try to explain to the crown prince that he is not a chicken. The king brings the most beautiful woman in the country to the dining room. For hours she talks to the prince but he continues to behave like a chicken. Finally a beggar asks whether he can have a try. The beggar crawls under the table and shoves against the prince and also begins cackling and flapping until the prince gets up and sits down on a chair. A friend told me this story. The friend had traveled from Lithuania to Berlin to study at the university. He was only seventeen. As a child he was already renowned for his learning. He enters the study house and the others inside immediately rise, his father and grandfather too. When he says a prayer no one around him dares to pray aloud. No one dares to say anything, except for asking others who have not yet noticed the child to be quiet. Although he registers as a student in Berlin he doesn't follow any classes. A large part of the day he sits in a café. When he orders something to eat he always asks the waiter whether he perhaps wants to try some of his food. Most waiters say no. A waiter asks whether he's afraid that the food is poisoned. When food has a strong smell it can make the one who brings it to the table unbearably hungry. That's why the law says that a slave or a waiter has the right to part of the food. The Lithuanian says that by following the law as precisely as possible someone finds the strength to act freely. I say that someone who wants to follow the law still has to pay attention to everything that's unusual or uncertain so as to decide whether the unusual or uncertain is covered by the law and thus how he has to behave according to the law. A good old Jew needs time and strength to follow the law. He needs the remaining time and strength to find out what might possibly not be covered by the law and he won't have anymore strength left for his freedom.

The Lithuanian says: the border of the law is not like the border between one country and another. Someone who fully exerting all his strength explores the border of the law no longer knows at which side of the border he finds himself; isn't that enough freedom? A border is a fault line, a crack looking for its own place. A border isn't the place of decision but decision the place of the border. A king gets angry at his wife. He writes a divorce letter and hands it to her. Immediately afterward he snatches it back from her hands. Each time she wants to marry someone else the king says: can you prove that you've divorced me? Where is your divorce letter? And each time she asks him for something he says: why would I give something to a wife whom I've already handed a divorce letter? Even before Heidegger comes to power the Lithuanian travels away from Germany. He says: I'm going back and I'll take a jester. I say: how will you find a jester? He says: I'll go pray somewhere. Once bystanders are gathering around to look at me I will suddenly point at one of them and appoint him as my jester. The new old Jews in Berlin hope that the Lithuanian wants to join them. A new old rabbi walks up to him while he's sitting with me in a café. The rabbi invites him to celebrate with the new old Jews. The Lithuanian says: what do you call the building where you celebrate? The new old rabbi says: the temple. The Lithuanian asks: is your temple a temple where you can dance with animals? The rabbi says: you're joking. The Lithuanian says: in your temple do you have an organ and when someone plays it does everyone who's there sing along like a choir of angels? Someone doesn't sing along but asks a question to someone sitting a few chairs down; is he asked to leave the temple? The new old rabbi says: the Jews visiting our temple are professors, doctors, lawyers, high civil servants. Some practice early in the morning, before joining their family to the temple, the prayers that they will sing in the temple that day. The Lithuanian says: when someone sits in between two others and his clothes are torn and he sings loudly and afraid, is he asked to leave the temple? The new old rabbi: someone will ask him to be quiet. The Lithuanian asks: and if he's not quiet? The new old rabbi says: in that case he's asked to leave the temple. The Lithuanian shrugs his shoulders. Before leaving Berlin the Lithuanian gives a party in the large hall of the temple of the new old rabbi. It is the cheapest place he could rent. There is herring and boiling hot tea. The Lithuanian has made few friends in Berlin. That's why he asks me to invite a few of my best friends. Everyone is dressed up as a Jew.

GONCHAROVA: You too?

BENJAMIN: I'm dressed up as Abraham. I'm wearing a dark suit, a shirt without tie, and a kaftan. A fedora on my head. Gershom comes as my wife, wearing a wig and a scarf. It's a good party. We leave the temple's outside doors open. Adorno climbs behind the organ and begins to play. As the evening passes more and more new old Jews and non-Jews walking on the street and hearing the music come in. They come in and take something to eat and to drink from the table. Then they pick a spot somewhere in the hall. They look around in expectation. They become so many that the Lithuanian and I and my friends start to feel uncomfortable and hardly dare to speak with each other. We leave the temple and walk to an all-night café. In that café we continued and closed the party. Someone forgets the law for five minutes. Someone doesn't think about the law for five minutes or he thinks about the law as if thinking about something that doesn't matter, a bunch of flowers in a vase, something like that, somewhere. And in those five minutes he performs the most hideous actions or could have performed the most hideous actions. Then he remembers the law again but the five minutes are now in the law. They can no longer be taken from it. He can inspect the law more carefully, he can interpret and expand the law, but the five minutes remain part of the law. He can do something terrible again and hope that he therefore becomes so inattentive that he is able to lose those five minutes in a way that he honestly no longer knows where he could find them again. He can even hope to be allowed to long for those five minutes like someone longing for something that doesn't matter.

GONCHAROVA: Is the show scary?

BENJAMIN: The show could also have been violent but I've chosen to do it as much as possible without violence.

MAIMON: That's a great relief.

BENJAMIN: An enormous arena with a dying man in the middle. Is that a violent show? Or several pairs of men dying, next to each other in two beds on little wheels. The audience can try to guess who will die first and has to encourage one or the other. One of them dies first. The other waits until there's a free spot next to another bed and then his bed is moved there.

MAIMON: Why do they die?

BENJAMIN: Anyone who feels that he'll die that very day can register. When he dies as the first of the two he receives a cash prize. He can surprise his heirs with a larger inheritance than they expected. The heirs may visit the dying man during the show. They may also visit the man in the bed next to him and give him to eat and to drink. They may rent nurses to take care of the other man. A day after the party the Lithuanian suggests to Adorno to prohibit all plays in which a god is mistaken because he doesn't pay close attention or in which a god cannot stop laughing. He is also against plays in which a god mourns a dead person. Then he suggests prohibiting young men from acting. Only old men who have drunk too much wine are still allowed to perform plays. Why not dying men?

MAIMON: And when someone doesn't die?

BENJAMIN: The show can take the entire day. After sunset they switch on the lights in the arena. The city is dark but the arena is glowing. The show only ends at midnight and when the last man in bed no longer seems to get any weaker. Assistants push the bed out of the arena. He often dies shortly after though. The impatient spectators throw cushions and fruit seeds at his bed.

GONCHAROVA: But the show is without violence?

BENJAMIN: When there's only one man left and it's still long before midnight a dying lion can be carried into the arena on a stretcher. The stretcher with the lion is put down next to the man's bed.

MAIMON: Do we have to fear something?

BENJAMIN: The chicken doesn't have to be afraid. What should the chicken be afraid of? Sometimes someone gets afraid that his feelings aren't strong enough. For example, that he doesn't feel sad or lonely enough because of someone he knew and who died. Sometimes someone tries to force someone else to feel or do in return in a way that causes someone to feel or to want to do even more. When that doesn't work someone sometimes wants to swing his arms around wildly in disappointment that his feelings or actions do not matter. This violence is a completely different kind of violence from the violence that has to do with wanting to embarrass bodies or genitals by saying: I don't have to be here. That's a form of idolatry.

MAIMON: Because genitals: who saw genitals bringing something to life, who saw two genitals bringing each other to life?

BENJAMIN: Half a chicken and a great scholar! Maybe you can help me to better understand how theater begins so we can end the theater in a better way? How does theater begin? From singing and dancing in a group? How do I imagine this? The most impatient singing dancer starts to speak and the remaining dancers let it happen? Should I begin differently? Someone tells a story. He moves his body. The movements come closer and closer to dancing. Instead of dancing himself the storyteller makes a small gesture and a group of dancers appears dancing and singing next to him. The storyteller puts on a mask when he tells what one of the figures from his story is saying. Then there are shows by two or three masked storytellers and one or two groups of dancers and singers. Old Jews cannot do this. When a Jew tells a story he cannot just put on a mask to say what God is saying. That would be idolatry. The spectator watches and listens to the play with all the attention he has. The attention is a promise that he can also be listened to and watched when something happens to him. The night after his visit to the theater the spectator finds it difficult to sleep. He only falls asleep when it's nearly light. Shortly after he wakes up and gets up. He doesn't feel hungry but still eats a big breakfast. Then he leaves for the theater again. The sun is shining but the air is still fresh. The first play begins. Half an hour break. The second play begins. Again a break. The third play. A break. A short play in which ridiculous cannot be embarrassing. Then the day has passed. A spectator living far away from the theater doesn't arrive home before the sun has set. What does he do when he's at home? Does he tell his slaves what he has seen? Does he tell his wife, if he has a wife? Does he lie down in bed and does he try to sleep? The next day he again sees four plays and again the day after. Each play that the spectator sees has never been performed before. The spectator cannot compare one show with another. How long does the spectator endure this? After several years the restagings begin and the plays without fear for the ending. Then dance and music separate from theater. What to do about it? Someone tries to put theater, music, and dance together again in a new-old whole. Royal gods and goddesses, with bodies too heavy to make large or high jumps, always moving along just a bit too late with the hidden musicians' music. By the way, the music is beautiful. When I hear it I want to sing along although I know that what I'm singing doesn't sound like music at all. At school I'm not allowed to sing along when the entire class is singing. The teacher covers her ears with her hands when she hears my voice among the other voices. Sometimes I try not to sing along with the music but to sing something back. Sometimes it just seems as if I'm inventing new music while walking around in the music piece that I'm listening to. Of course I know that my music isn't real music. Now and then I notice that I'm still listening to the first music, just like a walker in a forest only now and then notices that he's surrounded by trees. The first music seems to make you remember feelings instead of evoking them. As if the feelings preceded the music. Someone makes a play and all roles are for kings who cannot remember whether they can sing and dance. No one who sees the play is able to ask a good question about what he's seeing. Even later he isn't able to ask a good question about it. Another possibility: abolishing theater, music, and dance and making room for music arising from the movements of thinking how to act before and after doing so. The movements of justifying like when someone tries to justify a love. Listening to that music and moving. Walking back and forth to be better able to listen to that music. Lying in bed with someone and moving so as to be better able to listen to that music. Someone attentively watches something that he wants to have explained. He asks for music that helps to pay attention, even if the attentive one no longer hears the music and the music is an explanation but maybe not the only explanation. Maybe that's the music that fits the final state. It is my hope that the shows will be the birth pangs of the final music.

GONCHAROVA: How can someone abolish all music?

BENJAMIN: Movement becomes dance. Dance becomes ritual. An action has to be performed like such and such. Someone looks as if he may expect the ritual to end like he wants it to end. If it doesn't work can it be done again? If the world no longer existed, what kind of music would remind you of the world? Four scholars try to listen to the final music. One can no longer decide, one can no longer breathe, on can no longer hope, and one remains whole. The first scholar says that he doesn't want to marry because the law makes him happy like a wife would. A reward for obedience to the law is more obedience just like a reward for gladly touching a woman is even more gladly touching? The undamaged scholar says: aren't you afraid to become convinced of the correctness of a certain explanation while the majority acts in a way that is prohibited by your explanation or doesn't behave themselves in a way required by your explanation? Someone convincing his wife in his bedroom of something doesn't have to be afraid. Someone walks up to the undamaged scholar and says: the first scholar talks about the law and there's a circle of fire burning around him. The undamaged scholar asks: are his clothes on fire too? The undamaged scholar walks up to the first scholar and says: I hear that you're talking here about the law and that there's a fire burning around you; are you trying to sing a piece of text on the melody of the final music? The first scholar says: no, I was busy recalling pieces of text from remote parts of the law as if they were standing huddled against each other. The undamaged scholar asks: how do you determine whether a piece of text may stand next to another piece of text? The first scholar just cannot decide. The second scholar stands still in order to think. The undamaged scholar passes by, surrounded by a group of students. The undamaged scholar greets the second scholar but doesn't get a response. He greets him again but doesn't get a response. He greets him again and the second scholar finally greets him back with an excited and worried voice. The undamaged scholar says: I don't want to leave you alone before I've heard what you're thinking. The second scholar says: I'm thinking about the beginning. God floats just above the water. He uses all his power not to touch the water. Is He anxious that even the smallest part of Him will be immersed in the water? A few days later the second scholar can no longer breathe. The third scholar tries to listen to the final music and what he hears sounds so strange that he cannot imagine that the music could have anything to do with him. On a Sabbath he rides on a horse along the temple and tries to hum what he remembers of the final music. He notices that he cannot remember even the tiniest part of the melody and loses his remaining hope. One week later, again on a Sabbath, he walks to a place where a woman is standing who has her bed with her. The woman says: aren't you the third scholar? He bends over to pick a flower. The woman thinks that it is impossible that the third scholar doesn't know that it is prohibited to pick a flower on the Sabbath. The woman says: you're someone else. He offers her the flower. Only the undamaged scholar listens to the music and remains in one piece. Music never confuses the undamaged scholar? Or did the undamaged scholar fill his ears with wax before he and and his friends came near the music? Moses asks God whether the text of the law couldn't have been clearer. There are parts of the text that Moses doesn't understand well. God says that the text that Moses doesn't understand well refers to the music that belonged to the text and now has been forgotten. A scholar like the undamaged scholar desires the music and this strong desire helps him to find an explanation. Moses says: may I see it? Suddenly Moses is in the study house of the undamaged scholar, at the far end, behind the last bench of students. The undamaged scholar reads a difficult piece of text. Then he suggests an explanation. A student asks the undamaged scholar how he knows that this is the only correct explanation. The undamaged scholar says that this is the law as God has given it to a Jew. The Jew receives the whole law: law of the skin and law of the mouth. Then the Jew feels a kiss on his mouth. The Jew is left behind with the law of the skin and the beginning of the slow and difficult remembering of the law of the mouth. The explanation that I suggest here is like a memory of something that I pronounce every day in order not to forget it. Moses says: God, why did you give the law to me and not directly to the undamaged scholar. God says: be quiet. Moses says: I cannot speak well. Suddenly Moses finds himself on a square, in the middle of a crowd. The undamaged scholar is standing on a platform and his skin is peeled from his body. The flayed body is placed in a large tank of water. The flesh slowly becomes grey. Everyone goes home and at night Moses stays on the square. The next morning two men lift the body from the tank and carry it to the butcher's store. Moses follows them and sees how the undamaged scholar's body is put on the counter among the other meat. A man enters the shop and stops before the counter. The butcher says: anything else? The man says: be quiet. The butcher says: anything else? The man says: I was only taking a look. The butcher says: the animals are brought in early in the morning. I cannot delay the slaughtering because the first customers are already waiting in the shop. For the entire day I hardly have a moment of rest. Only at the end of the day I can eat something myself or read a book or talk to my wife. By then it is usually already dark. Moses says: to be able to listen better? Shall we start the show?

(Benjamin bows to Heidegger. Heidegger gets up. Benjamin pushes the desk to the back. Maimon and Goncharova try to help him. Benjamin moves the two chairs. Benjamin looks at Heidegger and gestures to one of the chairs. Heidegger sits down in that chair. Mrs. Heidegger enters and sits down next to her son. Finally the audience files in through the door.)

BENJAMIN: Welcome ladies and gentlemen. Welcome guests. Ladies and gentlemen, today we present you Salomon Maimon and Natalia Goncharova, freshly escaped from the Soviet Union. We also have among us the two expert commentators Martin Heidegger, Chancellor of the Third Reich, and his mother, Mrs. Heidegger. Do you hear me?
AUDIENCE: We hear you.
BENJAMIN: Do you hear me?

AUDIENCE: We hear you.

BENJAMIN: Listen. Is one of you in mourning?

AUDIENCE MEMBER 1: I'm in mourning.

BENJAMIN: You have to sit in a different chair than your usual one.

AUDIENCE MEMBER 1: I'm sitting on a different one.

BENJAMIN: Alright. Listen.

AUDIENCE: We'll do it and we'll listen.

BENJAMIN: Listen.

AUDIENCE: We're listening. We're listening well. Say it.

BENJAMIN: Listen.

AUDIENCE: Say it. Say it.

BENJAMIN: Salomon and Natalia have only recently met. I'll ask them what they feel for each other.

AUDIENCE: Ask it.

BENJAMIN: No, you ask it first.

AUDIENCE MEMBER 2: Salomon, what do you feel for Natalia?

BENJAMIN: Ask her too.

AUDIENCE MEMBER 2: Natalia, what do you feel?

AUDIENCE MEMBER 1: Is what you feel for him enough if he feels the same?

BENJAMIN: Enough for him or for her?

AUDIENCE MEMBER 2: If you lost him, for how long would you hope to find him again?

BENJAMIN: Now I would like to hear what the experts think of this. Martin Heidegger?

MRS. HEIDEGGER: What is my son supposed to think of this?

AUDIENCE MEMBER 1: You're his mother.

MRS. HEIDEGGER: I know what I'm talking about.

BENJAMIN: Alright. My apologies. Let's return to our couple. Natalia, what did you think when you saw Salomon for the first time?

GONCHAROVA: I thought that he would look more like a negro. I had heard that his great-grandfather was a negro.

AUDIENCE MEMBER 2: He has dark hair and blue eyes.

AUDIENCE MEMBER 1: Blue eyes?

AUDIENCE MEMBER 2: There's blue in his eyes.

(BENJAMIN WALKS UP TO ONE OF THE AUDIENCE MEMBERS, STOPS IN FRONT OF HIM.)

BENJAMIN: You look like someone who has learned from experience. May I ask you whether you've been married?

AUDIENCE MEMBER 1: I've been married.

BENJAMIN: And what did you experience?

AUDIENCE MEMBER 1: I cannot put it in words.

BENJAMIN: Still try to tell it. What do you feel when looking for words? Do you feel disappointed?

AUDIENCE MEMBER 2: Indignant?

BENJAMIN: Hurried? Do you want to laugh or cry?

AUDIENCE MEMBER 1: I'm not laughing, I'm not crying.

BENJAMIN: If I ask you to choose one of the two? You have to choose one of the two or else leave?

AUDIENCE MEMBER 1: Or else I have to leave? I'm not an actor.

BENJAMIN: Who says you are?

AUDIENCE MEMBER 1: Why then would I be able to laugh or cry?

BENJAMIN: Only actors can laugh and cry?

AUDIENCE MEMBER 1: And else I have to leave?

BENJAMIN: That's not what I'm saying.

AUDIENCE MEMBER 1: I cannot do it. I really can't do it.

BENJAMIN: Let me help you. Your wife tells you something you cannot forget?

AUDIENCE MEMBER 1: I really can't do it.

BENJAMIN: Your wife tells you that she'd rather have married someone else? You may find this so terrible that you cannot talk about it.

AUDIENCE MEMBER 2: Your wife becomes forgetful and suddenly no longer recognizes you?

BENJAMIN: Your wife tells you that her life has passed without her ever having lived?

AUDIENCE MEMBER 1: I don't know how to begin.

AUDIENCE MEMBER 2: Your wife burns the food?

AUDIENCE MEMBER 1: I find it terrible.

AUDIENCE MEMBER 2: Your wife only wants to lie next to you in bed when you have put on silk pajamas?

BENJAMIN: I don't want to make you cry.

AUDIENCE MEMBER 2: He doesn't cry.

BENJAMIN: Calm down. Maybe I'll get back to you later and then we'll try it again. Is that alright?

AUDIENCE MEMBER 1: I cannot do it.

AUDIENCE MEMBER 2: He cannot do it?

AUDIENCE MEMBER 1: I'm about to cry but I cannot cry.

AUDIENCE MEMBER 2: Sometimes I don't understand why someone weak and useless has a soft and friendly face.

AUDIENCE MEMBER 1: How long do think you could bear hearing me cry?

BENJAMIN: Tell him something nice so he feels better.

AUDIENCE MEMBER 2: I don't think he'd bear it for long.

AUDIENCE MEMBER 1: If I began to cry now I would feel so lost.

BENJAMIN: Maybe it's better to return to our couple.

AUDIENCE MEMBER 2: It's a beautiful couple.

BENJAMIN: And you Salomon, what did think when you saw Natalia for the first time?

MAIMON: That she looked Jewish.

BENJAMIN: Maybe we can start again with Natalia.

AUDIENCE MEMBER 2: Good girl.

AUDIENCE MEMBER 1: Great girl, do you dare to show yourself with him, near him?

GONCHAROVA: Isn't that what I'm doing?

AUDIENCE MEMBER 2: Do you dare to be alone with him?

GONCHAROVA: More and more.

AUDIENCE MEMBER 1: More and more!

BENJAMIN: Can you lie next to him and not get aroused?

AUDIENCE MEMBER 1: What a question.

BENJAMIN: Salomon, can you lie next to her and not get aroused by her quietly naked body, large and gracious, generous when she's generous?

AUDIENCE MEMBER 1: The one who rightfully amazed and warmed by her own radiance is honestly ready to move around him in honest calm and silence.

AUDIENCE MEMBER 2: Sometimes you can speak well.

BENJAMIN: Which body part would you give up not to be banished from her?

MAIMON: Which body part of mine or hers?

AUDIENCE MEMBER 1: Body parts? Arms and legs?

MAIMON: Mine or hers?

BENJAMIN: Not to be banished from her?

AUDIENCE MEMBER 1: Give up?

BENJAMIN: You enter the house and all children crowd at the door to greet you first? Or you're sitting in a chair and all children sit around you and look at you and they all have exactly the same face as you. Not the face you had when you were as old as them but the face you have at that moment. One of them leans against the light switch making the light in the room constantly switch on and off.

MAIMON: My children?

BENJAMIN: A man is counting children. Another man walks up to him and asks: are these your children? It's not alright to count someone else's children.

MRS. HEIDEGGER: Who's counting children here?

AUDIENCE MEMBER 1: An excellent question!

BENJAMIN: Maybe we should put this question to a vote.

MRS. HEIDEGGER: Do you hear a song in your heart?

BENJAMIN: A good question. Natalia, do you want to give him a kiss?

AUDIENCE MEMBER 1: Say what you want to do.

BENJAMIN: You may think about it. Take your time. Do you need as long as a song? Could you maybe sing a song?

AUDIENCE MEMBER 2: Which song?

BENJAMIN: Should I say which song?

AUDIENCE MEMBER 1: You could make a suggestion.

BENJAMIN: Natalia, do you want a particular song?

GONCHAROVA: I wouldn't know which song.

BENJAMIN: Maybe the song of the bird that got a bit confused? Or maybe the song of the musicians at the wedding?

AUDIENCE:
Trumpeter points with trumpet
To clarinetist who points with clarinet
To violinist who points with violin
And he doesn't make a sound.

But points and looks
Like someone who jokes but he doesn't
Joke and like someone who makes disappear
But he doesn't make disappear.

Trumpeter asks with trumpet
To clarinetist who asks with clarinet
To violinist who asks with violin:
Is that all you make disappear?

Or did I at first
Not notice something
And now it is gone
And now it is gone?

BENJAMIN: Did that take long enough? Or do you find it difficult to think with all these people around you?

GONCHAROVA: It doesn't make it easier.

BENJAMIN: You may also give a kiss and while you're kissing think whether you want to kiss him.

AUDIENCE MEMBER 1: You may kiss him slowly.

BENJAMIN: Maybe she wants someone else to try the kiss first. Natalia, do you want two members of the audience to try the kiss for you?

AUDIENCE MEMBER 1: I would like to do it for her.

(Audience member 1 pretends to kiss.)

AUDIENCE:
Is that all
That you make disappear?
Or is there something
I didn't notice at first?

AUDIENCE MEMBER 2: And now it's gone?

MRS. HEIDEGGER: No one knows how I feel today.

AUDIENCE: No one.

MRS. HEIDEGGER: My husband is in the book, my son is sitting next to me, silent. No one knows how I feel.

AUDIENCE: No one.

BENJAMIN: Mrs. Heidegger!

MRS. HEIDEGGER: I can scream but I won't.

AUDIENCE: Good girl.

BENJAMIN: Can we return to our opening question?

MRS. HEIDEGGER: I could yell and cry.

AUDIENCE: No one know how she feels.

MRS. HEIDEGGER: What does my day look like? I wake up, walk to the bathroom to wash myself. I drink a glass of fruit juice. I read the newspaper as if newspapers were soon to go out of style. That's the amount of attention with which I read the newspaper. I go outside. Sometimes I shop. Then it's time for lunch. I visit my son or I pay a visit to a friend. Then it's time for supper. Then it's evening. Then it's night.

BENJAMIN: Let's return to the couple. What do you want to see?

AUDIENCE MEMBER 2: A kiss.

BENJAMIN: What kind of kiss?

AUDIENCE MEMBER 1: From her to him. The first kiss that comes to her mind.

MRS. HEIDEGGER: I don't agree. If she doesn't want to kiss she shouldn't kiss. Were you about to kiss him? Would you kiss him now if no one had asked for it?

GONCHAROVA: I don't think so.

(Mrs. Heidegger gets up and offers Heidegger her arm. Heidegger gets up too. Mrs. Heidegger stands still for a moment.)

MRS. HEIDEGGER: Natalia, please join us for a moment, if you like.

(Mrs. Heidegger, Heidegger, and Goncharova move to one side of the room, as far from Benjamin and Maimon as possible.)

BENJAMIN: Why is the show not working? Because the audience isn't good enough? Because the host isn't good enough?

MAIMON: I don't know what you could have done better.

BENJAMIN: Because the questions and answers haven't been prepared enough? Or still too much? The audience consists as much as possible of persons who have never attended a show before. Sometimes someone says it's only the first or second time hoping to be allowed to take part again.

(The audience walks from Benjamin to Mrs. Heidegger.)

MRS. HEIDEGGER: Did you ever meet Stalin?

GONCHAROVA: Not really. I've only seen him from far away.

MRS. HEIDEGGER: Stalin's got it easy. Stalin can trust anyone but whom can Martin trust? In the fifth year of his government Martin became so disappointed that it became dificult for him to talk with others. I suggested to Martin to take a cruise along the Greek islands. I also invited some of his and my acquaintances to join us. The two married couples who used to live in the houses left and right of the house in which Martin was born. They're still living there. Martin's aunt, my sister, also joined us with her husband and children. Two of Martin's high school friends. The wife and children of one of the friends. I thought it was unfortunate that Martin didn't have a girl to bring along. Especially in the weeks before our departure I sometimes pointed someone out saying to Martin: I didn't know she was so beautiful, but he didn't look or he looked and didn't say anything. The highlight of the trip was our visit to Delos. From far away the island was like a marble palace, surrounded by water.

AUDIENCE MEMBER 1: Mortals call the island Delos.

AUDIENCE MEMBER 2: But immortals looking upon the island from above call it the blue sea's brilliant star.

MRS. HEIDEGGER: There were two Jews living on Delos. They had heard when the ship would arrive and were waiting for us on the quay. They were dressed in dark red cloaks with pointy hats on their heads. The ship was too big to moor at the quay. We dropped anchor just outside the surf and a small rowing boat brought us to the shore. The Jews made deep bows and moved their arms slowly back and forth in a solemn way. We stayed on the island for less than a day. Martin bought me a scarf. In the evening we returned to the ship, which that night remained anchored at the shore. The island was lit by a full moon. The next morning we continued our journey. Sometimes dolphins swam along the ship for a while. Martin threw them bread and they jumped out of the water to catch it with their mouth. Can you imagine?

GONCHAROVA: Very beautiful.

MRS. HEIDEGGER: One evening I asked Martin to read to me from the book of the dead. Martin is good at that. Slowly the sky above the sea got darker. We could hardly recognize each other's faces anymore. There was no sound except the waves and Martin's voice. The captain had ordered to shut down the ship's engine. After a couple of minutes Martin said that it was too dark to continue reading. One of his childhood friends undressed and jumped overboard because he felt like swimming. The captain had a long rope tied to his waist with the other end tightly fastened to the ship's rail. The childhood friend dove into the darkgrey water. Eventually he emerged with a small writhing fish in his outstretched hand.

GONCHAROVA: It must have been beautiful.

MRS. HEIDEGGER: I would have liked someone like you to have been beside him. I can already see you walking beside each other and stopping at the entrance of my house. I greet you and you greet back and finally, suddenly, he also begins to speak. Although he's always spoken to me, you know. Martin, you've always continued to speak to me, haven't you?

GONCHAROVA: I've heard his voice on gramophone records. The speeches.

MRS. HEIDEGGER: But then there's no need to remain silent to her, is there? She's just like me. Say something to her. Natalia, say something to him so he can say something back.

GONCHAROVA: What should I say?

MRS. HEIDEGGER: Say what comes from your heart.

GONCHAROVA: I am happy to be here.

MRS. HEIDEGGER: Maybe you can now look at each other.

(The audience walks to Benjamin and Maimon.)

AUDIENCE MEMBER I: They marry.

BENJAMIN: Suddenly someone notices that he is being mistreated and at the same time he recognizes that situation to be more real than the preceding ones, no matter how much he resists it. Suddenly someone is made sick. Suddenly a part of how someone sees himself is taken away from him. Not everything at once but it is clear that that could have happened as well. Moreover there are the ones who see it happen. Some say that it makes them sad. Some say that they feel concerned about the feelings of the ones they are watching. Some try to help. But it's made clear that all of them could also have turned against him and could have happily assisted in making clear what's happening to him.

MAIMON: The old Jews think so?

BENJAMIN: What does this have to do with the old Jews? This has nothing to do with the old Jews. Do you want to know the look in someone's eyes who embraces you when you're crying? Heidegger didn't expect Hitler to step down at all. Really.

MAIMON: Stalin would like to know what Heidegger has said or done. He is afraid that what happened to Hitler could happen to him.

BENJAMIN: Stalin only had to ask. He could have called me.

MAIMON: What did Heidegger do?

BENJAMIN: Martin moves his arm inattentively and his hand touches a globe standing on the floor next to his chair. The globe begins to spin. Hitler says that he's proud of his collection of globes and world maps. He gets up and picks up a globe standing next to the cabinet and puts it on the desk. It's not a regular globe but a flat earth spinning around its axis. Hitler explains that all the land and the mountains and hills are represented on one side of the earth and all oceans and lakes on the other side. The part of the earth's surface that is not covered by water is much smaller than the part covered by water; that's why the scale on one side is smaller than on the other side. Then Hitler opens a desk drawer and takes out a stack of maps. He carefully unfolds one of them and places it on top of the desk. I try to recognize the contours of countries or coastlines but I don't see anything that appears familiar. Hitler says that this is the rarest map from his collection. He points to a text in one of the map's upper corners and asks whether I can read what it says. I shake my head. It says: Jews live here. They sleep while sitting on their horses. Because they don't have any other animals except horses they don't eat meat and they don't drink milk. Hitler asks: a patient traveller? I say: a patient traveller travels to a place that is not marked on the best of maps or is at most only an assumption. He travels through a desert or across an ice sheet and is not disappointed when he arrives tired or hungry and everyone he knows is already there.

MAIMON: And Hitler puts his cap onto Heidegger?

BENJAMIN: Hitler is silent for a moment. Martin looks at him. Hitler looks at Martin. The telephone rings. Martin sits closest and picks up the phone, out of fear or out of habit. It is Gershom Scholem who wants to talk to me asking me impatiently how the conversation is going. I hand Hitler the receiver. Gershom remains silent. Hitler remains silent. Hitler places the receiver on his desk without ending the conversation. The receiver is heavier than usual. Hitler looks at me and then looks at Martin for a long time. I hear Gershom screaming hooray through the telephone. Hitler wipes his face with a large handkerchief and says he needs rest so that he can recover what he's feeling. Hitler asks: how is Moses' death? Does something happen to Moses that you don't dare to tell me? I say: Moses hears the angel of death approaching him. Moses says: don't disturb me, can't you see that I'm writing? The angel asks: what are you writing? A letter? The angel of death comes up to Moses carrying a gravestone in his arms. The angel of death asks Moses whether he wants to write a text on the gravestone. Moses says: what do you need a gravestone for? The angel says: may I help you? The angel writes with his finger on the stone: "Here Lies." Moses says: it's a very small stone. The angel says: this gravestone is buried along with the dead. The gravestone is meant for a grave that's as light as the counterweight of a promise. The angel of death tries to cover Moses' face with his shadow. Moses is fast and strong and with small moves he constantly manages to turn his face away from the shadow. Then Moses gets up and walks in the direction of a mountain. The Jews ask each other what Moses is up to this time and follow him. He climbs faster and faster and disappears in the thick fog. The Jews can no longer see him and walk back. Moses reaches the top of the mountain and looks around. Then he suddenly feels a mouth forcing open his own mouth. At the bottom of the mountain the Jews burst into tears. No one knows the location of his grave. Hitler says: is it prohibited to bury Moses? Hitler picks up the receiver again and asks Gershom about the location of Moses' grave. Gershom says: no one knows the location of his grave, not even Moses himself. No one has shown Moses the location of his grave. Once history has come to an end the dead wake up in their graves and dig their way underground to Jerusalem. Moses wakes up too and starts to dig but he doesn't know the location of his grave. Moses is the last one to arrive in Jerusalem. The other dead have enough time to prepare a festive welcome. Hitler picks up the cap and places it on Martin's head. I walk to the doors and throw them open. Hitler's bodyguards enter, hesitating when they see Martin wearing the cap. Martin looks bewildered too. Hitler tells the bodyguards that Martin is the new chancellor. Gershom screams through the phone: life and health to Heidegger! The bodyguards repeat after him. Then I say it too and put down the receiver.

MAIMON: Is that the Jewish conspiracy?

BENJAMIN: Oh no, these are things that you cannot plan.

MAIMON: So there's no Jewish conspiracy?

BENJAMIN: We talk with each other. Sometimes we make proposals to each other. Horkheimer, Adorno, Gershom, myself, and sometimes a few others. Marcuse has an uncle who's a pharmacist. During the day he produces and sells regular medication but at night he tries new mixtures. He's an honest man who first tries each mixture on himself. The pharmacist gives Marcuse a couple of white pills and tells him that they help to change or cancel differences. Marcuse shows us the pills. He suggests to dissolve the pills in the Berlin tap water, Gershom asks: difference between what and what? Each of us takes a pill and swallows it. Days later Horkheimer and Gershom are still nauseous. Adorno's hands are covered in small wounds and bruises. Adorno recalls that he has invented and made the most overwhelming music but he cannot remember the music itself. The others cannot remember hearing the music either. We gather once more in the same room and this time only Adorno takes a pill. Every few minutes he bangs on the table with his fist or open hand. After half an hour we've had enough and leave him alone in the room. The following day we meet each other in a café. Adorno says: how can someone make new music? Inventing new music that rejects the usual and waiting until a custom arises to explain and supplement the new music? Inventing new music and explaining and supplementing it with old music? Where can someone find an old custom? In folk music? How can folk music help the Jews to make new music? Because the Jews don't have their own folk music, at most a few borrowed tunes. Maybe the Jews can first make late folk music and then new music? When does someone make late work? When someone is desperate to find something again while it's still in front of him? Maybe the Jews can be brought to a place where they have to stay until they begin to make late folk music. On a Sunday we drive in a large car to a music festival in the countryside. Horkheimer is driving. The festival takes place on an estate. In front of the estate owner's home there is an elongated lawn with the stables on one side and on the other a wooden shed in which the music performance is taking place. Men and women have come with their children, also small children in buggies. The entrance is free. After each round of applause the doors of the shed are opened. New listeners may come in. Tired listeners may get up and sit outside on the grass. On the grass there's a stand with food and drinks. The people on the grass still hear most of the music. When we arrive there's a string quartet playing. During the next round of applause we get in but the string quartet has finished its performance and it's time for a break. We again look for a spot on the packed lawn. After the break we choose chairs on the last row, close to the exit. On a low stage there is a piano and a large vase with flowers. A young woman climbs onto the stage. Two long braids of dark brown hair rest on her back. Gershom gives me a nudge and says: let's go outside. I get up and after a brief hesitation the others follow Gershom and me. Just after we've managed to close the doors behind us the woman begins to play the piano. A few weeks later Gershom suggests to lend money at a high interest rate. He even took the trouble to write a song to accompany it. He gives the song to a singer and the singer makes a gramophone record of him singing the song. Then also another singer and then another one and another one. A singer hardly earns enough money to afford his daily groceries. There are many singers living in Berlin. A singer lives in a run-down house. When he exercises his voice his neighbors come and complain that he's waking up their children. His wife has left him. He writes her letters but cannot send them because he doesn't know her address. He waits and hopes for that one song that will make him a rich man. The singer cannot write a new song himself. He has to wait until someone else writes a song for him or suggests an unused song. A song he can sing in a way that every listener wants to sing it in his place. He is ready to buy the song from any angel. The usurers' song is such a song. Dear sirs, if you want and you remember, the usurers' song?

AUDIENCE MEMBER 1: They marry.

BENJAMIN: Someone sees someone for the first time while hearing this song. He runs to the radio when he hears the song again. He raises the volume and says: listen, they're playing our song.

AUDIENCE MEMBER 2: They marry.

BENJAMIN: But first the usurers' song. If you would be so kind.

AUDIENCE:
By lending
We trade in time
That's not ours
But God's,

That is theft.
We give
To whom doesn't have
And the next day

We ask it back double,
Also to ourselves,
A decent Jew wants God dead,
God's parties have understood this well.

(Mrs. Heidegger walks up to Benjamin and Maimon. Heidegger stays behind with Goncharova.)

BENJAMIN: Someone sees a profit for himself that leads to someone else's loss. The profit is so small that it would be embarrassing for someone to openly ask for the profit but it is difficult not to close one's hand around the small profit. Like a tired mouth around a kiss. What is a small profit for a poor man? The undamaged scholar says that a poor Jew has to be treated like a rich man who has lost his possessions and has forgotten that he hasn't given up the hope of ever finding them again. Someone tries to be inattentive in order not to see a small profit or loss. Someone may be ashamed because of this inattentiveness. Someone may marry because of this shame. From what can this be deduced? What is sufficient ground for a divorce? The impatient one says: the only sufficient ground is that the woman does what is embarrassing, that she shares a bed with another man because she wants to and doesn't mind whether a witness sees her in that bed. The patient one says that it is already enough if she burns the food. Or when her voice is so loud that the neighbors can hear her when she's speaking in her own house with her husband. The undamaged scholar says that it is enough if he sees a woman somewhere whom he finds more beautiful than his wife.

AUDIENCE MEMBER I: They marry.

BENJAMIN: A man has two wives. One has the same name as the other. He writes a divorce letter in which he mentions the woman's name but no other characteristics by which the woman could be recognized. He gives the letter to an envoy. The envoy gives the letter to one of the wives. Is the divorce valid? A man has two wives. He writes a divorce letter addressed to the first woman who comes out through the front door of his home. He gives the letter to an envoy who waits at the front door until one of the women comes out. Moses asks the angel of death: on which day were you made? The angel says: on the first day, directly after it became light. Moses says: the first man is made and you've already had five days to prepare yourself to kill him, is that fair? The angel says: the text of the law lies ready before I am made. The text of the law tells about a man who dies in a tent. I have five days to study the law before the man is made. I haven't slept for a moment. Moses says: a man writes a divorce letter and then he enters his home and asks his wife for something to drink, a glass of tea. She brings him a glass of tea. He takes a sip and says: I no longer want to stay married to you; here is a divorce letter. She says: what did I do wrong. He says: the tea is lukewarm, not warm. She says: you had already written your divorce letter before you came in.

AUDIENCE MEMBER 2: What are they doing?

BENJAMIN: When a man is weak of mind he may not divorce. Even when he's drunk. A deaf-mute may only divorce his wife if he was already deaf-mute at the time of the wedding. Otherwise he may not divorce. A weak-minded man asks a woman who's crying: shall I embrace you? The woman says: your embrace is rather strong. A divorce letter is not valid if the man writes the letter on the woman's hand. A divorce letter is not valid if the man gives the woman the letter but at the same time says that the paper on which the letter has been written remains his. A marriage is already a marriage when two people are lying together in bed and are not embarrassed when witnesses see them.

MAIMON: In a bed?

BENJAMIN: How would a bed made by God or grown by itself look? Of course it doesn't have to be a real bed. They also don't have to lie down. A man may divorce his wife if her skin is rough to the touch. Also when her breath has a sour smell. He may not divorce her for these reasons if he has said before that her skin and breath don't matter to him. If the man's skin and breath are repulsive she may ask for a divorce letter. If she has said before that it doesn't matter to her she may say: I thought that it didn't matter to me but now I notice that I cannot bear it. A king's wife embarrasses the king. He wants to prevent this from happening to him again. He asks his first minister to bring him a new woman every day. The king marries the woman in a hurry. He sleeps with her and immediately afterward he hands her the divorce letter lying ready next to the bed. The woman says: did I do something wrong? The first minister has to write a new divorce letter every day and place the letter on the floor next to the king's bed. Everywhere in the kingdom one can hear the crying of divorced women feeling lonely. No one dares to marry a woman who's previously been married to the king. One day the first minister's daughter asks her father to bring her to the king. The next day the first minister writes a divorce letter in which his daughter's name is mentioned and then he brings his daughter to the king. The king marries the daughter and sleeps with her but even before he is able to reach for the divorce letter she says: does the king think that there is a difference between a story and the same story told by a wife to her husband?

AUDIENCE MEMBER I: They marry.

BENJAMIN: Someone is constantly surprised by infidelity by which he doesn't want to be embarrassed. That's why he works day and night on the text of arrangements with his lover.

MRS. HEIDEGGER: He's just saying stuff. That's what I told Martin from the beginning.

AUDIENCE:
Someone should
Not let wait,
Someone should
Place a hand

In a hand
And take
A hand
In a hand.

Saying and
Not doing, no one
Wants to wait
For that.

BENJAMIN: Mrs. Heidegger, I have the highest regard for your son and for you. Truly. I would consider it an honor if you wanted to be my mother.

MRS. HEIDEGGER: He calls it an honor.

BENJAMIN: I honestly mean it.

MRS. HEIDEGGER: He's making insulting jokes.

BENJAMIN: May I offer you my apologies if I have ever insulted you or your son in any way?

MRS. HEIDEGGER: My son can say for himself what he thinks of it.

BENJAMIN: Nothing gives me as much pleasure as hearing your son speak.

MRS. HEIDEGGER: He's just saying stuff. Don't listen to him. Give him five minutes and he's just saying stuff. Do you see him washing a frightened old lady?

BENJAMIN: I would be very willing to wash you.

MRS. HEIDEGGER: I'm not afraid.

AUDIENCE MEMBER 1: They marry.

(Heidegger and Goncharova walk up to Benjamin, Maimon, and the audience. Mrs. Heidegger takes a bouquet of flowers from a vase standing beside the desk and gives it to Goncharova.)

MRS. HEIDEGGER: These flowers are for you.

GONCHAROVA: Will he speak to me?

MRS. HEIDEGGER: Of course he will speak to you. Martin, say something to her.

AUDIENCE MEMBER 1: He walks next to her as if he might say something to her at any moment.

AUDIENCE MEMBER 2: That's walking, not saying.

AUDIENCE MEMBER 1: As if there are words in his heart.

AUDIENCE MEMBER 2: Words that are only in the heart aren't words.

GONCHAROVA: When he's angry at me, what will he do?

MRS. HEIDEGGER: He will sing a magnificent song for you.

GONCHAROVA: When he's tired, what will he do?

MRS. HEIDEGGER: He will say that you're water and that he wants to drink.

GONCHAROVA: When he's tired of me?

MRS. HEIDEGGER: Is water ever tired of water?

GONCHAROVA: Will he speak to me?

MRS. HEIDEGGER: Martin, say something to her. Tell her something. Something that puts her at ease.

AUDIENCE:

Be silent. Don't explain.

How I am is

Yours. Don't explain.

It doesn't matter. Be silent.

In the heart
Of the sea I say in my heart:
Why afraid? Didn't I say: my heart
Belongs to who sets boundaries to the sea.

(Mrs. Heidegger walks to the cupboard, takes out the book.)

MRS. HEIDEGGER: Martin, here you go. Just begin some-where. So she can hear your voice. One line is already enough. I could try to imitate your voice but it would sound different though.

(Heidegger looks at his mother. Mrs. Heidegger opens the book.)

MRS. HEIDEGGER: I can give it a try. Wagoner, Anton, died 1908, old age, Fritz-und-Clara-Haberstrasse 17. Wagoner, Nikolaus, died 1925, fall from window, Von Hofmannst-halstrasse 35. Wagoner, Franciscus, died 1939, lung disease, Von Hofmannsthalstrasse 35.
AUDIENCE MEMBER I: They are married. We were there.
MRS. HEIDEGGER: Thank you. Is it enough?
GONCHAROVA: It's enough. What else can I say?
AUDIENCE MEMBER I: Your home is my home, your silence my silence, my death is where your death is.
MRS. HEIDEGGER: What else can a mother desire to hear?
BENJAMIN: A mother can burst into laughter.
MRS. HEIDEGGER: Just go win the war.
BENJAMIN: Are they married?
MRS. HEIDEGGER: Go win the war.
BENJAMIN: What should I bring you when I've won the war? A piece of perfumed soap?
AUDIENCE:

What a delight.
The cow and the chicken
Are on a business trip.
Will later be your job too.

What will you want?
Bread for your children
And clothes for your wife.
And for your whole life you'll hear

The music played
On your wedding day.
Like the cow and the chicken
Dancing in their beds far away.

(A piece of paper flutters to the ground. Audience member 2 picks it up and unfolds it. He waves his left arm.)

AUDIENCE MEMBER 2: It's a telegram.

BENJAMIN: A letter from heaven?

AUDIENCE MEMBER 2: A telegram for Mr. Heidegger. From the rabbi of Birobizhan, Moscow.

MRS. HEIDEGGER: Don't know him.

AUDIENCE MEMBER 2: The text is as follows. I felt myself swelling with happiness when I received word of your marriage. A good wife opens the gate to the garden so you can come in and go out. She is the gate, garden, and banishment at the same time. A Jew...

MRS. HEIDEGGER: A Jew?

AUDIENCE MEMBER 2: A Jew says that the first woman is necessary for the animals. Of each species there is a male and a female animal but they don't know yet how to deal with each other. God wants the man to make it clear to them. God makes the man and tells the animals that they have to watch the man. The man looks as if he's lacking something but he doesn't know what. Then God puts the man to sleep and makes the woman. The animals surround the man and woman when the man wakes up. They push each other out of the way to have a better look at how the man notices the woman lying next to him and how he touches her. The animals then imitate the man and the woman. A male animal looks as if he's lacking something. A female animal comes up next to him and he looks as if he just woke up. Then he touches her. If it were up to me everyone would have to marry as soon as possible. Allow me to congratulate you from the bottom of my heart on the occasion of your marriage.

MRS. HEIDEGGER: I thank the rabbi.

AUDIENCE MEMBER 2: What is the color of the sky when the man lies down to sleep for the first time? As blue as the sea. What is the man dreaming of when he is sleeping for the first time? I wish that each time you sleep next to your wife it is like the first and the last time. I wish you this as if you two were the only ones who want the night never to end. That there's no morning but that the night continues. What is the magnificent color of the sky when the man wakes up next to the woman for the first time?

BENJAMIN: This is a telegram in which every word counts?

MRS. HEIDEGGER: What are you still doing here?

plain

(A plain between Berlin and Jerusalem. A blazing, almost blinding sun. Benjamin and Maimon standing next to each other. The light dims. They take a few steps toward an entrance gate.)

BENJAMIN: It was my idea first to conquer Poland and Lithuania and maybe Belarus and the Ukraine. The study houses of Bialistock, of Slobodka, of Brisk, of Telz, Dvinsk, and Kamenitz are spitting out hundreds of old Jews. With all those brave old Jews you can easily conquer the world. The brave Jews can take part in the army of the lords of the exodus. A recruit may choose any name for always. He may try the name for a day or a few days. If he doesn't like the name he can return to the registration officer and enter a new name. The registration officer writes down the new name.

MAIMON: Is it usual to promise something?

BENJAMIN: No, but go ahead.

MAIMON: What is usual?

BENJAMIN: It is not unusual to promise that you want to forget your right hand before forgetting Jerusalem. Try that.

MAIMON: Before I forget Jerusalem I want to forget my hand.

BENJAMIN: Considering a certain place more important than another place is very close to idolatry.

MAIMON: You said it first.

BENJAMIN: Go wash your hands.

MAIMON: Where do I find water?

BENJAMIN: If there's no water you may also wash your hand in earth or in air. Don't make stains on your uniform. Instead of washing your hands you may also give someone a hand over and over again. The old Jews may enlist in the brave army. Or they may live in a camp. The camps have been built close to villages that hardly anyone has ever heard about.

(Maimon washes his hands in the air. Benjamin washes his hands in the air too.)

BENJAMIN: In this region you often only have to move a few hundred meters away from a village to find a forest that no one dares to enter or a plain that no one dares to cross. When someone asks a villager why not he says: bears, or he says: wolves. An old woman no longer leaves her home and when someone asks her why she says: I'm tired of the smell of lions and bears. There are also many old Jews living in the villages who visit another old Jew if they feel even the slightest bit frightened. The other old Jew is sitting in his room. The visitor talks about himself, holding the compensation for disturbing him in his hand. Whatever the other old Jew says or does may be explained as counsel and as explanation of the law that is applicable to the visitor's case. The more the other old Jew wants to study in fear the worse he is able to endure the visits. It becomes more and more difficult to persuade the visitors to end their visits. They continue to pose new questions while the line of visitors in front of the room becomes longer. They ask more and more unimportant questions. What should I give my wife for her birthday?

MAIMON: Are there any musicians in the army?

BENJAMIN: An army without musicians? How can they walk long distances? They have no instruments but they are the first ones that begin to sing when the others haven't sung for a while. The musicians are also the ones who during a battle help to carry dead and wounded soldiers off the battlefield. A few days before an important battle they dig holes in the ground. The soldiers aren't tired yet. At the beginning of the war we let the Jews from the camps dig the holes so the Jews in the army can rest. But it is too complicated to transport the Jews from the camps to and from every battlefield. Moreover the presence of the Jews from the camps disturbs the Jews in the army. They say: let the Jews from the camps dig their own holes. They dig the holes in the fields just behind the front, not far away from the place where the battle is expected to take place. If there's little time they dig a couple of very large and deep holes instead of many small holes. The soldiers arriving last to take part in the battle see holes left and right of the road. They stop singing. They go on and one of them begins to sing again and everyone sings along, louder than before.

MAIMON: How do the Jews in the camps die?

BENJAMIN: There are no man-eating birds flying in the air above the camp.

MAIMON: There are man-eating birds?

BENJAMIN: Not here. There is no court in the camp that may condemn someone to death. And even if there were such a court it wouldn't be easy to decide that someone has done something that causes him no longer to be allowed to live. The court has to consist of twenty-three judges. The smallest majority is insufficient to condemn someone to death. The majority has to contain at least two judges more than the minority. To prevent the court from condemning someone to death with the decisive vote being cast by a god dressed up as a human. The court needs to interrogate the witnesses separately. The witnesses not only need to have seen the prohibited action but also have warned the accused that the action is prohibited.

MAIMON: Is there music in the camps?

BENJAMIN: The first group of Jews to arrive was told that they would be called together each morning to be counted and warned. In the evening, after work and before supper, and finally one more time before midnight. As far as I know these assemblies have never taken place. The counting and warning are more like a prayer than a blessing. The prayers belonging to certain moments may only be said once during those moments. Someone says the afternoon prayer and suddenly remembers that he has said the afternoon prayer once before on that day. He immediately stops praying, even if he's halfway through a sentence. A blessing can be said at any moment of the day. The aim of someone saying a blessing is unimportant. But he may only bless if he thinks that there is an occasion for the blessing. A prayer without an intention is no prayer. Someone can prepare himself for saying a prayer by looking for a right intention. How much time does someone need to prepare himself for a prayer? Someone needs longer than a day to prepare for a prayer that he has to say every day; how does he have to live? Someone says a prayer and has the feeling that no one can hear what he's saying, no matter how loud he prays. He can try to study so intensely that he forgets to pray at the prescribed moments. If he continues to feel worried he can study the text of the worrisome prayer instead of the text of the law. Someone doesn't need to have an intention to study. Intention dissolves itself in studying. So studying looks like saying a blessing over that which is not present. When the women in the camp want to study they may study. The world to come is near. When a woman doesn't want to cook she and her husband can eat in the canteen. When their clothing is worn out they can choose new ones from the clothes in the warehouse. Every couple of weeks there is a truck delivering a pile of secondhand clothes collected in Berlin and in other cities. The camp is like a garden and like the heavenly assembly. In heaven scholars wake up late, eat breakfast, study with each other all day, and each one tries to convince the other that he's dead. Whoever lets himself be convinced falls to the ground as if dead. At the end of the day that day's winners pick up the fallen ones, carrying them to the dining hall. The day's winners tell the fallen ones: wake up, get up. In the dining hall Friday supper is served every day.

MAIMON: But there's no tree.

BENJAMIN: The tree is an unimportant piece of stage decoration. A non-Jew says that someone who dies changes into a wolf. He also says that the moon is the sun's uncle. They are no Jews. Other non-Jews say that someone who dies changes into a star. Did you ever hear about non-Jews thinking that someone who dies changes into a tree? In the beginning God arranges the garden. A plant over here, an animal over there. The first man looks like God but without crown and without wisdom and without victory or brilliance or justice or beauty and all the other ornaments. God asks the man to give names to everything he sees. That's fun for an afternoon. Whatever the man says, it's always fine. Then God makes a woman. How does the man tell the woman how beautiful she is? Does she know the names that he gave to the animals? Does she understand what he says and when he says that she's like a gazelle? Or does the man tell the woman the names of the animals by pointing at an animal and then telling the woman that she is graceful like a gazelle or majestic like a lion? Then the goddesses appear. First to God and then to the man and the woman. What is happening? The man and the woman string leaves together and hang them around their bodies. God asks: are you trying to look like trees? God says that they have to undress. Then He slaughters a few of the animals standing around the man and the woman. He tells the man and the woman that they may use the slaughtered animals' skins as clothing. Another story. God remembers the old goddesses and hardly anything else. He is furious and has pity all over the place because He cannot remember well the reasons why He's feeling like this or this. He speaks with someone and the next day He no longer recognizes him or confuses him with someone else. Immediately after making the world He has already forgotten the names of the plants and animals. That's why the man has to give all of them new names. God doesn't want the man to give new names to the tree of life and death and the tree of good and evil. He wants to have time to remember their names himself. When the man nevertheless gives the two trees new names he is chased from the garden. The man calls one tree "Little Tree" and the other tree "Dear Tree." God is forgetful like a man who lies in bed with his woman and who constantly stops touching her and asks: shouldn't we introduce ourselves first?

MAIMON: What happens to the animals after the man has been sent away from the garden? Do they also have to leave the garden?

BENJAMIN: It is dusk and someone stands next to an animal in a field. The tree is unimportant. The animals are also not really necessary. Do you see any animals around here? Or do you think that the animals hid themselves in the ground fearing that else they would be sacrificed? The man and the woman have two sons. The first son likes to sit on the ground and digs with his fingers through the soft earth. The second son calls the animals together and leads them to a field. When they have eaten up the field he walks in front of them to another field. An animal stays with the first son. The first son shares his food with the animal. Sometimes the animal sleeps with its head against the first son's body. The first son talks to the animal when something has happened to him or when he thinks that something has happened to the animal. He speaks so often with the animal that it is impossible that he hasn't promised the animal something during one of these conversations. The second son takes the animal away from the first son and slaughters it and burns it. A couple of days later the man and the woman ask themselves why their sons stopped visiting them. The man goes to look for his sons but he doesn't find them. He notices that the animals are suddenly afraid to look at him. He returns to the woman and for the first time in a long while he again sleeps with her. This story is like something that someone remembers and wants to repeat over and over because even after so many times he still isn't sure whether he is allowed to remember it. Someone sees a large man suddenly punching another man in the face. The man falls to the floor. A second large man kicks the man in the stomach and then in his face. Someone walks up to them. The first large man walks toward him. Someone stands still and says: you're beating him to death. The second large man continues to kick the man on the ground. Someone looks around to see whether there's someone else who can help. The first large man says: it won't take long. Another story is that the first man and woman also immediately feel anger and desire and shame but the feelings pass over the entire garden like storms and everyone in the garden, the humans and also the animals and the trees, and maybe God himself, bend in the same direction. God is sitting in the garden and notices that the way in which He thinks about Himself is moved and deformed by storms and floods as if He hasn't kept a promise. He appoints his Jews who have to deflect all fear and shame and jealousy from Him so He remains quiet and clear.

MAIMON: Early Jews?

BENJAMIN: Before the world is made the law exists. How does the law exist? As a whole of rules that's so perfect that it needs no explanation? Or as the simplest form of a rule, something like: if this then that? Or merely the simplest form of "if"? Another story is about the sixth day. In the first hour God decides to make the man. It is morning. A couple of stars are still visible in the air. The birds are noisy. In the second hour He speaks with angels about his decision and He studies the law. The angels say no; the law says yes. The angels say: why would you make a man; are we not enough for you? If you want to give someone the law, why don't you give the law to us? God looks at the angel of death and says: on the first day all angels come to me asking me what they have to do. I say that they can sometimes do small tasks for me and that otherwise they may sing. I also say that I don't want to hear them sing for the first six days. The other angels surround the garden and practice their singing without making a sound. You're sitting outside their circle on the ground. You cannot see the garden and you're reading the text of the law. You have been able to read for nearly five days. Did you find a good reason why I wouldn't give you the law? The other angels look at the angel of death. The angel of death is still holding the text of the law in his hands but doesn't know what to say. In the third hour God gathers the clay. In the fourth hour He sculpts the clay into the shape of a man. In the fifth hour He makes the skin around the clay. Skin is important. In the sixth hour He sets the man upright. In the seventh hour He lets him breathe. In the eighth hour He allows him to enter the garden. For slightly less than an hour the breathing man doesn't live in the garden but isn't sent away from the garden either. What should he have answered had someone asked him at that moment: where are you? In the ninth hour God tells him what he is allowed to eat and what he's not allowed to eat. In the tenth hour the man is disobedient. Between the beginning of the ninth and the end of the tenth hour the man meets the woman. They barely have the time to get to know each other well. Even during their first bashful encounter there are still animals passing by that the man needs to name. The woman says: just close your eyes for a moment so we can be together quietly. But the man doesn't dare to close his eyes and while caressing her perfect skin he continues to look over her shoulder mumbling: you are a koala, you are a rhinoceros, you are a gazelle, you are a wildebeest, you are a springbok. The eleventh hour is the hour of the court session. The evening is cooling down. In the twelfth hour the man and the woman are sent into the night. Some angels think that this is the moment that they have to start singing aloud. God points to a few singing angels and the singing stops immediately. Then God points to the other angels one by one. He points to the angel of death last. The man has lived in the garden for barely three hours. He hasn't been allowed to celebrate a single Sabbath in the garden.

MAIMON: The man and the woman are sent away from the garden but what is there outside the garden? A desert? Are there already animals? Or are they sent away together with the man and the woman?

BENJAMIN: The animals are allowed to pass the Sabbath in the garden. The man and the woman have an empty first Sabbath. The day after the first Sabbath God makes new angels and lets them drive the animals from the garden. Another story. The first man is large and beautiful but he can neither speak nor hear. God shows him how and the man imitates Him. They walk from tree to tree and God picks a fruit and acts as if He's eating. Then the man eats. The old goddesses surround the man so that he can no longer flee and then they tear him apart. God and the woman are watching. Had they intervened they would have been torn apart too. Then God collects the shreds of body and splatters of blood and makes from them the second man. The second man is incomparably less than the first one. When God and the woman look at each other they remember the most horrible thing they've ever seen. God and the woman no longer want to touch each other. God sends the man and the woman away from the garden. Another story. God withdraws Himself into Himself and through this contraction He makes place for the world. The original light spreads itself together with time across the new world. The original light is like the final music. It helps to pay great attention. The light spreads and then collects itself in storage vessels that aren't large enough and shatter into pieces. From the fragments the world as it currently exists arises. Some fragments contain more light than others. Some say that there's only a single storage vessel and that the first man, who cannot speak, is this original storage vessel. The whole world and also the second man, the man who sleeps with the woman, have arisen from the fragments of the shattered body of the first man. Another story. In the beginning there are two types of light: the thoughtless light and the light with which the world is made. Freedom is someone's shadow in the former light and responsibility is someone's shadow in the latter. The first man is so big that his shadows touch God everywhere. According to another story, in the beginning the ten jewels lie in God like ten grains of sand in the water of an ocean. A single grain of sand keeps the ocean restless. That grain of sand is justice. The ocean withdraws itself to get rid of justice. Justice is set free and diffuses itself across the world that is made through that diffusion. All other jewels are released too and become storage vessels for justice. The storage vessels shatter into pieces. Another story. Because God withdraws Himself into Himself justice is released. The law accompanies justice like time accompanying light. The law diffuses across the world and then withdraws into itself. Due to inattentiveness this second contraction allows uncleanliness to be released. This uncleanliness diffuses across the world without being accompanied by anything. In the world to come men may finally touch women as if they can study the law without fear and still study well. In the world to come the difference between rules that are connected to certain moments and rules that are not will disappear too. MAIMON: No Jews.

BENJAMIN: The Jews will come later. God is sitting and the goddesses are dancing around him. God becomes afraid that each movement He makes will become part of the dance. When He notices that a part of his body has moved to the rhythm of the dance He shouts that He's not dancing but studying. To tease him the goddesses shout back: what then? Which question? Whether one of us loves you? Or doesn't love you? Or whether you're just enough toward the Jews?

MAIMON: Is justice an old goddess?

BENJAMIN: How can you think something like that? The old goddesses are someone's feelings toward someone else. Feelings that someone can ask about: do I feel more for that one or that other one? Do I feel more pity for the first or the second? Someone can be just or unjust but can someone be more just toward the first than toward the second? Something can also be more or less unclean than something else. There's unclean that continues to make that which comes closer or touches it unclean and there's unclean that doesn't make unclean but there's no more unclean or less unclean.

MAIMON: Isn't justice a blindfolded goddess? In the large court room of Moscow there are two statues of justice. Both of them are blindfolded. The larger statue is standing in the public gallery, in a niche behind the last row of visitor chairs. The smaller statue is standing to the side of the president of the court. The breasts look round and soft. The garment she's wearing looks very thin and light. When I was expelled from theater school and suddenly had a lot of free time I sometimes went to a court session. After the theater ban so many people want to attend court sessions that it becomes difficult to find a seat in the public gallery. Early in the morning there are already long queues in front of the entrance of the court. During the night some visitors sleep in sleeping bags on the pavement in front of the court to increase their chances of finding a seat the next morning. There are also visitors who give the guards money or other gifts.

BENJAMIN: All old goddesses have been blindfolded and tied up together. The royal gods want to dream of God being tied up in a wrong spot. God remembers what has happened and what is going to happen, in any case until the beginning of the world to come. Someone shouts that the world to come has begun. God's memory of earlier and later events is still complete but He is suddenly afraid that He no longer knows the difference between before and after. To hide His confusion God acts as if He is sleeping and dreaming. God dreams that the royal gods are performing a play and invite God to attend the performance. They know that God feels uncomfortable when He is sitting on a chair stuck for a long time between other chairs on which others are sitting. Afterward they ask Him what He thought of it. As bad as you thought? Or maybe less bad? I thought it was going rather well tonight, don't you think? Maybe this is also a dream of the royal gods. Who dreams something like that? The old goddesses try to take care of a Jew and raise him. The Jew speaks too loud or he is indignantly silent. An old goddess says to God: we give the Jew something, a beautiful sweater or a pair of shoes, and maybe he is happy for a moment but then he walks away again or asks immediately for something else. He cannot focus his attention on the same thing for even a minute. One of us stays the whole day with him and then he hardly seems to notice when she's leaving. She asks whether he wants to wave her goodbye and he says no. She asks whether he wants to give her a kiss and the Jew turns his face away from her.

MAIMON: Do old goddesses sleep?

BENJAMIN: They can also wait.

MAIMON: Do old goddesses speak with each other?

BENJAMIN: Maybe they prefer to send envoys. An old goddess sends an envoy to another old goddess.

MAIMON: Do old goddesses dream?

BENJAMIN: It is very unlikely that they dream, even if they're lying on their backs blinking their eyes toward God. God is sitting on His judge's chair between the old goddesses' beds. God easily gets nervous when He is on His judge's chair. When God loses faith in the power of justice He can try unbearable pity or another feeling that is so strong that it can no longer be directed toward another person and no longer has anything to do with the old goddesses' power. He can try it with undirected, all-engulfing, oceanic love. Someone has made a list of eight other types of love: love that causes the receiver to continue to live and die without needing more love and love when giver and receiver don't know about each other's love and love when the giver knows but the receiver doesn't and love when giver and receiver know of each other but that the receiver didn't ask for and love that the receiver did ask for and love that is less than the receiver asks for but that is given with a happy face and love that is given with a sad face. Each of these types of love may be weak or strong. If love is strong enough someone may sleep on the tip of a sword. With how many lovers can someone sleep on the tip of a sword? A giver and a receiver fearfully resemble each other. The giver loves the receiver but another one only has to appear in the vicinity of the receiver and the giver begins to love that other one too, as strongly or as weakly as he loves the first receiver.

Someone pities someone else. He wants to know whether he can feel love for the same person at the same time. Does he feel so just that he can receive pity and love like guests who have forgotten that they are guests? Sometimes pity is so strong that the receiver cannot but feel at least as much pity for the one who pities him first. So pity goes back and forth until both are full of pity for the ones they pity, and there's no longer any place for anything else. God can also try it with all-engulfing shame. Then He sits down on the chair of shame. Oceanic shame is the shame someone feels because he could have been present while a man embarrasses another man. After the end of history the humans and animals, and even the plants and mountains and hills, are engulfed in justice and pity and love. The old goddesses dance around like elegant retarded girls. Each day is Sabbath. God doesn't work, doesn't make fire, doesn't bring anything from one place to another. He studies so cautiously that no other world is made.

MAIMON: God studies alone?

BENJAMIN: When I imagine the final Sabbath I think that he has a study friend. But I cannot imagine well what that study friend would look like. Maybe it's the chicken. What else does the chicken have to do in the world to come? Lying down to sleep next to the butcher? Crossing the road and being embraced by a sobbing man?

MAIMON: Did the rabbi from Lithuania, your friend, have a jester?

BENJAMIN: If you were my jester I would hit you because you're getting old too fast.

MAIMON: Sweet jester or bitter jester? Oceanic jester?

BENJAMIN: A jester who is suddenly kissed by a king?

MAIMON: A jester who has suddenly been kissed by a king?

BENJAMIN: Someone has felt so much love that he thinks

that he can no longer feel love or no longer needs to feel love. Is this the opposite of oceanic love? God floods the world. With what? With water. Before the world is flooded a man hears that he has to build a ship, so many meters longs, so many meters wide, so many meters high, with a roof and without sails or oars. The man hears that he has to build a ship and he plants the trees that he wants to use later for wood. It takes at least a hundred years before the trees can be cut. He builds the ship on the peak of a rocky hill, on the edge of the desert. Passersby say: for whom is this enormous coffin? He says that it's a ship. They say: your ship maybe floats on quiet waters but as soon as waves start the ship will surely capsize and sink. The rain begins to pour down and the man takes shelter in the ship, together with his wife and his sons and their wives. In the ship there is room for two animals of each species. There is also room for seven pairs of the animals that are appropriate for slaughtering. How does he choose the animals? He has a list with the names the first man has given to the animals. He calls the names and lets the first animals who remember their name enter. Some animals have children with them but the children are not allowed in. They don't say goodbye to their children fast enough and a next pair of the same species is called in. The world is covered with water. The first days all the animals are seasick. After a week everyone is used to the ship's movement on the water except the lion. The lion lies on the floor in a corner of his room and says that he holds the other animals accountable. The other animals don't understand why the lion is angry with them and they assemble in the middle of the ship. One animal says: what can we do to get the lion to reconcile with us? The fox says: I know three hundred stories that I can tell him to get him to reconcile with us. The other animals say: go to him. The fox takes a few steps. He says: I have forgotten one hundred stories. The other animals say: you still have two hundred stories; shouldn't that be enough? The fox takes few other steps. They say: now what? The fox says: I've forgotten another hundred stories. The other animals say: you still have hundred stories left, shoudn't that be enough? The fox goes on. But when the fox is standing in the lion's room he says: I've forgotten all stories; let everyone reconcile himself with the lion on his own. The man brings the animals the food that they're used to eat and at the moment of the day or the night at which they're used to eat. The man doesn't sleep for the entire year. One day he is so tired that he forgets to feed the lion at the usual time. Later he suddenly remembers the lion. He runs to the lion but even before he can put down the food the lion jumps up and leaves his teethmarks behind in his arm. On the ship he talks to no one, not even to his wife. She says: why did you take me along?

MAIMON: A good question?

(A train arrives, old Jews get out, looking around as if their eyes need to adjust to the light.)

MAIMON: There are the Jews.

BENJAMIN: At the end of time God is sitting in a room and one after the other just person comes in to tell Him that he's doing so well and that he's feeling so well.

(The old Jews walk hesitantly in the direction of the entrance gate. They stand still before Benjamin and Maimon.)

OLD JEW I: I see that you're wearing a uniform. Are you a

civil servant? If I may ask you something, did we get out at the right place?

BENJAMIN: A nice uniform. Who looks best remains longest in one piece.

OLD JEW I: It is a beautiful uniform. It must have taken years of work. There was no conductor on the train. Some of us were afraid that we would get out at the wrong place.

BENJAMIN: You've gotten out at the right place. The world to come is nearby.

OLD JEW I: And then?

BENJAMIN: Each animal may be eaten and slaughtered in any way.

OLD JEW I: Who's thinking about eating?

BENJAMIN: The animals are playing with each other. The chicken and the wolf and the lion. They come together and ask: shall we play temple?

OLD JEW I: I don't see any animals around.

BENJAMIN: Everyone feeling the smallest and vaguest feeling in himself is immediately able to sing in a miraculous and moving manner. And the songs don't disturb each other. You know how it goes?

OLD JEW I: It goes?

BENJAMIN: How it goes when every Jew prays aloud at his own speed and according to the melody he remembers. At the moment that all prayers sound together like beautiful music the listener knows for sure that he has arrived in the world to come. But in the world to come there's no praying.

OLD JEW I: Why would anyone pray in the world to come?

BENJAMIN: In the world to come the doors are opened by singing. When you're praying you may make as many gestures as you want. You don't have to be afraid that by exaggerating a gesture you're making the gesture ridiculous or that you're ridiculing someone with the gesture.

OLD JEW I: How to continue? Through the door?

BENJAMIN: Gentlemen, just a moment. My colleague would like to address you briefly. Mr. Maimon, I ask you to speak.

MAIMON: Now? I didn't prepare anything.

BENJAMIN: Just speak. Think of a chicken on Friday afternoon hesitating whether it will lay an egg. The chicken is slaughtered clumsily and may not be eaten afterward.

MAIMON: An egg?

BENJAMIN: Don't talk to me. Talk to them.

OLD JEWS: Did he say Stalin?

BENJAMIN: I said Stalin, so what?

OLD JEWS: Stalin will win. For us.

BENJAMIN: For you Stalin will win?

OLD JEW I: For whom else will he win?

BENJAMIN: Stalin will win for you. You're waiting for it?

OLD JEW I: He has had all his portraits destroyed. There no portrait left of him anywhere in Russia. Previously Stalin had given the order that his portraits should resemble him as little as possible. But also those portraits he found too painful.

BENJAMIN: Gentlemen, please forget Stalin for a moment. My colleague has something to tell you. Maimon, please, hold your speech.

MAIMON: Dear Jewish gentlemen, I welcome you.

OLD JEW I: He is very friendly.

BENJAMIN: Maimon, you're sounding too friendly. Think about chickens as if you descend from chickens. Can you manage?

MAIMON: I welcome you to this camp. You may stay here until you decide to serve in the army.

OLD JEW I: Or until Stalin comes to help us.

MAIMON: I wouldn't count on it. You may bury your dead.

OLD JEW I: We don't have any dead.

BENJAMIN: Maimon, I thought you had a better mouth. The camp isn't poorly furnished. There is enough paper in every toilet. You didn't need to collect newspapers before you came here. When someone no longer has enough strength to turn on his side he may lie on his back. You may sometimes grab his hand or put a hand on his forehead or breast. Someone can no longer speak but you think that he would like you not to leave the room until he is dead. Even when you hardly know him you may start to think of him as a friend. You may think of him as of a bride, not your bride but the most glorious bride you have ever seen asking you whether you want to be her witness because she has no more time to find someone else. For whom is it embarrassing when someone tries to convince someone else that he is in so much pain that the other wouldn't be able to handle the pain? Someone tries convince someone else that he is so happy to see the other that the other wouldn't wish anything else but to be as happy? If you hold a finger in front of the mouth and nose and no longer feel any breath you may place and light two candles at the head of the bed.

OLD JEW I: May I choose my own bed to sleep in?

BENJAMIN: You may wash the body with warm water and dress it in clean white clothes. You may fill a pillow with unused earth and place it under the head. You may bury the body so that the deceased doesn't have to be ashamed because passersby see his body rotting and falling apart. Even when someone has said before his death that he doesn't want to be buried you may bury him when he is dead. You may say: I want a damaged text of the law to be buried together with me. I want my coffin to be carried to the grave next to the bier carrying the text. I want the funeral procession to make a small detour through a desert. Someone says: I don't want to be mourned. Does he think he's a god? Maybe he thinks that gods and animals will mourn him? You may bury as much as is left of the body.

OLD JEW I: Why wouldn't there be a whole body left?

BENJAMIN: Someone may lose a part of his body during his final disease?

OLD JEW I: Then this part can be buried together with the rest of his body, right?

BENJAMIN: A lion could have eaten half of someone. Or do you want to bury the lion together with the rest of the body in a coffin? Fine with me. You may rip your clothes. You may cover all the mirrors in the camp with sheets. You may mourn for seven days. Three days frenzied with grief, four days in deepest mourning.

OLD JEW I: We may mourn?

BENJAMIN: When you think that you may mourn you may certainly mourn.

OLD JEW I: As long as we want?

BENJAMIN: As long as you think you may mourn. God calls for Moses. An angel runs to God and says: Moses has been buried today. God asks: how does a king mourn? The angel says: the king rips his clothes. God rips his clothes. God asks: then what? The angel says: he sits and cries. God cries. The angel says: please don't cry, let me cry for you. God says: if you don't let me cry I will withdraw to a place where you cannot enter and I'll cry there. The angel asks: for how long? God says: longer than a day.

OLD JEW I: And then?

BENJAMIN: Thirty days and the eleven further months of the year and all years on the anniversary of the death, as long as you want. When one of you dies the one who mourns him most carefully may go live in Paris. The world to come would begin immediately if everyone would mourn well. Nothing more is needed. Just like two subsequent Sabbaths, executed with sufficient care, would be enough. Because of the dignity.

OLD JEW I: Whose dignity?

BENJAMIN: Who has dignity except for you and me and madam Sabbath? When a mourning man walks back from the funeral of the one he is mourning and he chooses the wrong road all other funeral guests follow him. Because of the dignity. Even if it is a muddy detour or a road through a place that makes unclean. It is allowed to jump across open or full graves to greet a Jewish king.

OLD JEW I: You're not only well-dressed but you also speak as if you have the best in mind for us.

BENJAMIN: You may comfort a mourner as soon as the funeral has taken place. It is shameful to visit a mourner while the dead body still lies with him, except when you come to help wash and dress the dead body. If you visit the mourner during the first three days you may not greet him and if you accidentally do greet him he may not return your greeting. If it is Sabbath you may however wish him a good Sabbath. When you cannot comfort a mourner you can visit a sick person. You may visit and watch a sick person a hundred times per day.

OLD JEW I: We're not sick.

BENJAMIN: When you're visiting a sick person you may talk with him and do something for him. You prepare food for him or you sweep the floor of the room in which he is lying sick. You can also help him wash himself. And if the sick person is sick of love? You talk with him but you don't do anything for him that he can do himself. When you cannot visit a sick person you can also visit someone who is old and has prepared himself not to become immediately desperate when he loses something.

OLD JEW I: None of us is sick at the moment. We are all in excellent health.

BENJAMIN: When the sick person is sick of pity? You talk with him for a long time and then, when he's tired of talking, you let him see or hear something beautiful. And when the sick person is sick of justice? You may turn your face to the wall when you think that you're dying. So as to forget what as slowly as possible? You're sick and you're afraid that your sickness will change you so much that you are ashamed that your wife stays with you until you're dead. You tell her that you want to divorce her. She says that she doesn't want to leave you alone. You take out a divorce letter. She says: that's really not necessary. You wave the divorce letter back and forth. She runs outside. You wait a bit and then you walk after her. The outside door is still open. She's standing on the other side of the road in the pouring rain. You say: I want to die immediately if you don't want to divorce me. She says: you don't hear what I'm saying. Her wet hair is stuck to her face. You may allow her to embrace you. You die in a remote city and you're afraid that your wife isn't allowed to say that you're dead. You may invite two witnesses so they can later help your wife to prove that she's not an abandoned woman. She may remarry, even with one of the witnesses. You leave on a journey and a man visits your wife saying that he was with you when you died. He says that there was no second witness. The witness marries your wife, and then you return. You write her a divorce letter and the witness writes her a divorce letter too. If you violate a prohibition you may think about a peace sacrifice. When you know that it is possible that you have violated a prohibition you may think of an uncertain guilt sacrifice. You've got two wives. You remember that the previous night you slept with one of them but you cannot remember with whom. The next morning you remember that you weren't allowed to sleep with one of them. You bring an animal to the temple and tell the priest: this animal is an uncertain guilt sacrifice. You return and the wife with whom you were allowed to sleep walks up to you and says: last night you were with me. You run back to the temple. The animal is being slaughtered when you arrive at the temple to tell the news? The slaughtering is not interrupted. The slaughtering has not yet begun? You don't get the animal back. The animal is brought to a field where a herd of animals is grazing. It remains in the herd until it gets sick or maimed and is no longer suitable as a sacrificial animal. Then it is sold and the temple receives the selling price. An animal also becomes unsuitable to be sacrificed when a man worships it. A man buys a piece of land and digs a grave in it in which the animal fits.

OLD JEW I: We have no animals. Do we need to catch animals?

BENJAMIN: A grave is like a tent. A camp is a like a field.

OLD JEW I: I thought that we weren't allowed to take animals on the train. Should we have brought animals?

BENJAMIN: You may banish animals instead of slaughtering them. You may banish cows, maybe goats, or sheep or pigeons. You may take two animals that are so much alike that you cannot keep them apart. You may then put two notes in a bowl and on one it says: "the first one," and on the other: "the last one." You may squeeze your eyes shut and take one of the notes from the bowl. Then you walk to the animals and wait until one of the animals walks up to you first. If you have picked the note "the first one," you chose this animal, if not the other animal. You can write a new note and tie it to the animal's neck with a red string. You may write on the note: "I've been chosen fairly." You may also anxiously stare at the sky fearing that animals banished from another world will land close to you.

OLD JEW I: We know that the sun is but a small star among many other stars.

BENJAMIN: A man has two wives. Each wife sends him a message stating that she's in bed and doesn't want to die alone. May a man run from one bed to the other? The man finds someone who is able to put on the man's clothes and act as if he is the man. May he ask an actor to remain with one of the wives until she's dead? Is that only allowed if he also finds a second actor to sit next to the other wife's bed? One of the wives dies. May the man now enter the other wife's room to take the sitting actor's place?

OLD JEW I: None of us has more than one wife.

BENJAMIN: A group of Jews is surrounded and they cannot escape. They are asked to choose and surrender one of them. It is better that they all die rather than choose someone. If they are asked to surrender one of them, and his name is given, then he may be surrendered to save the others. If a Jew in the group knows the rule and the others don't and he's not the one they ask for, may he tell them about the rule?

OLD JEW I: Are you trying to warn us of something?

BENJAMIN: Two witnesses visit your wife and tell her that you're dead but she doesn't allow herself to be persuaded. She may not remarry until your dead body has been found. It is not enough if she recognizes the clothes in which the dead body is dressed. It is possible that you have lent the clothes. If you have lost something it remains yours until you're desperate to find it ever again. As soon as you're in despair the finder becomes the owner. When may someone assume that you're in despair? When you tell witnesses that you think that you will never find it again. When you have lost it a long time ago in a spot where many people walk by. How long ago? After a year someone stops mourning; isn't that year long enough to begin to despair? What is the shortest possible time in which someone may begin to despair? The time that's necessary to ask someone how he's doing? You may also begin to despair when the water of the sea has swept along what you've lost. When a dead body has washed ashore and your wife finds it but the face has been erased?

OLD JEW I: Are there witnesses here?

BENJAMIN: A wave casts your clothes ashore and the next wave a naked man's body with an erased face? What may she recognize the body from? A missing finger is insufficient. A hand with two missing fingers and two extra fingers on the other hand? May she be certain that he's dead? A divorce letter directed to the your wife and written on the body with indelible ink?

OLD JEW I: Are you talking about us?

BENJAMIN: Your wife thinks you're dead. She says: what should I do? I cannot even bury him. A court allows burying an empty coffin if that helps her mourn. She walks behind the coffin. The children carry the coffin. The coffin is so light that one of the children can lift up the coffin with a single hand like a waiter lifting up a tray with cutlery. It is a beautiful funeral but there aren't many guests.

OLD JEW I: We're not desperate.

BENJAMIN: Gentlemen, in front of you lies the camp. Maybe you'll find a lion there. When he asks you for meat, give him bread. When he asks you who made it for you, then tell him that it was a Jewish woman. When he asks you which laws you follow, tell him. When he asks you how you'll die, try to answer that question.

OLD JEW I: May we also choose another question?

BENJAMIN: If it's a good question.

OLD JEW I: May we sleep with our wives in one bed, the ones of us who have a wife?

BENJAMIN: Why not? You may wash your sheets on Friday so you can sleep in a fresh bed on Friday night. You may deal with your wife as if she's a captured wife. You may let her undress, cut her hair, take a bath, mourn whom she has to mourn. When it's a beautiful day and you've got time you can sit down with your wife somewhere in the sunshine.

OLD JEW I: What is not allowed?

BENJAMIN: You may do what you usually do.

OLD JEW I: May we bike?

BENJAMIN: You don't have to be afraid that someone you see tells you that you look like a Jew, not even when you're saying a prayer.

OLD JEW I: Which prayer?

BENJAMIN: Any prayer you can remember.

OLD JEW I: What is absolutely not allowed?

BENJAMIN: What would you like to do?

OLD JEW I: Act?

BENJAMIN: You're joking.

OLD JEW I: During the long train ride we've worked on a play. May we perform it?

MAIMON: I thought the old Jews were against theater.

BENJAMIN: What kind of play is it? A tragedy? A comedy perhaps?

OLD JEW I: May we show you the play? It isn't dangerous. It is a passion play about the patriarchs Abraham, Isaac, and Jacob.

BENJAMIN: A tragedy?

OLD JEW 1: A tragicomic passion play, a pastoral play if you want, partially in verse. Only if you want.

BENJAMIN: If you keep it short.

(The old Jews divide themselves into two groups. They quarrel about who belongs to which group. A large Jew goes to one group and is pulled to the other group by three small Jews. Finally the first group takes up a position on the left of Benjamin and Maimon, and the second group on the right. The old Jew 1 and the old Jew 2 are part of group 1.)

OLD JEW 1: Your children will be numerous.

OLD JEW 1: Your children and your children's children and their children and their children will be numerous, so numerous that they cannot be counted.

OLD JEW 1: Your children and your children's children and their children and their children will be numerous, so numerous that fathers and mothers no longer know who their sons and daughters are.

OLD JEW 1 AND 2:

He who distinguishes the holy from the unholy,

That he may misplace all proofs of guilt,

And no longer be able to find them back in the sand

Or among the stars that become visible at nightfall.

OLD JEW 1: So numerous that they cannot be counted.

OLD JEW 2: That they cannot be described with a number.

OLD JEW 1: That their amount cannot be compared to a number

OLD JEW 2: That their amount cannot be compared to something that can be converted into a number.

OLD JEW 1: It is impossible to say about them: there were

so and so many and now they're all gone.

OLD JEW 2: How can Abraham's children and his children's children be numerous if he doesn't have a son?

OLD JEW 1: How can they be numerous if Abraham gets up early in the morning and takes his son with him to a mountain top to make a burnt offering?

OLD JEW 2: And the son asks: where is the sacrificial animal?

OLD JEW 1: He cannot believe it's happening to him.

OLD JEW 2: How old is Isaac when it happens to him?

OLD JEW 1: Is Isaac a small child or a grown man?

OLD JEW 2: Then Abraham goes to buy land for a grave.

OLD JEW 1: A grave for whom?

OLD JEW 2: Then Isaac, Abraham's son, goes to buy land for a grave.

OLD JEW 1: A grave for whom?

OLD JEW 2: Then Jacob, Isaac's son, goes to buy land for a grave.

OLD JEW 1 AND 2:
Each time the one catches the other,
The father the son, the son the father,
When the one buys more land to bury the other,
The one who's caught says: it's just a joke.

OLD JEW 1: They buy all the land.

OLD JEW 2: Enough land.

OLD JEW 1: So much land the stars in the sky and the sand beside the sea can be buried in it.

OLD JEW 2: So much land that no one ever needs to be dug up to make space for someone else.

(A Jew from group 2 lies down on the ground, another Jew from group 2 takes place at his feet.)

OLD JEW 2: There's Isaac standing at the grave of his father, Abraham.

STANDING JEW/ISAAC: Goodbye father is an old joke, always useful for a goodbye.

LYING JEW/ABRAHAM: What else to have a father for?

OLD JEW 2: What else to have a father for?

STANDING JEW/ISAAC: It's just a joke.

OLD JEW 1: There lies Abraham.

OLD JEW 2: Is he dreaming?

OLD JEW 1: Abraham doesn't dream because he could dream of the road up the mountain?

OLD JEW 2: Isaac doesn't dream because he could dream of the road down the mountain?

OLD JEW 1: But is Jacob, Isaac's son, dreaming?

OLD JEW 2: Each night he sleeps Jacob dreams?

OLD JEW 1: Isaac has two sons. Jacob and another son. The other son walks through the fields and over hills and mountains. Animals gather around him and press themselves against him. Jacob stays at home and tries to study. What is Jacob studying? His father's and grandfather's story. Isaac is sitting in his tent, blind, waiting for the next visit of the other son. Jacob enters and says: there is something I don't understand. May I ask you a question? When did you become blind?

OLD JEW 2: Isaac is blind but if the sun is shining he knows exactly when it is midday. He goes out and feels when the sun is shining straight down. Someone else has to tell him when it is nightfall.

OLD JEW 1: Jacob enters the tent. Isaac asks him whether it has become evening. Jacob says that the sun has set. Jacob says: there is something I don't understand well. Your father says that it is time for your wedding. He sends out a slave to choose a wife for you. You're not able to choose because you're already blind? The slave returns with a wife. Your wife sees a man walking toward her. Can she see that you're blind from the way that you're walking toward her? Jacob says to his mother: it is as if he doesn't want to speak with me at all. His mother says: dress up like an animal, that will please him. Jacob dresses up like an animal and reenters his father's tent. In the tent he sits down next to his father without saying a word. His father says: did you study too hard? Go sleep somewhere.

OLD JEW 2: Jacob says to his mother: he says that I have to go sleep somewhere. His mother gives Jacob food for on the road. He walks the whole night and the following day. At nightfall he arrives at the top of a mountain. Jacob lies down and falls asleep.

OLD JEW 1: The next morning Jacob continues his journey to his mother's brother. He has two daughters. The youngest daughter has beautiful eyes. He marries the older daughter and a week later the younger.

OLD JEW 2: Jacob hears that Isaac has died and travels to his father's tent to bury him. The other son has already buried Isaac. The other son says to Jacob: if you want we can bury him a second time.

OLD JEW 1: Does Jacob dream during every part of the night?

OLD JEW 2: How many parts does the night have?

OLD JEW 1: For Jacob the night has three parts. During the first part he sleeps with his face turned toward his first wife, during the second part with his face toward his second wife. During the first part he dreams about the road up the mountain, during the second part about the road down the mountain, during the third part about holding on to a body with all his strength while at the same time forgetting and remembering the body.

OLD JEW 2: How can the night's parts be distinguished?

LYING JEW/ABRAHAM: At the beginning of each part of the night there is roaring like a lion.

STANDING JEW/ISAAC: How can someone know that it is exactly midnight?

OLD JEW 1: No one can look up at night and determine from the color of the sky or the stars that it is exactly midnight.

LYING JEW/ABRAHAM: Someone can suspend a musical instrument from a string above the bed in which he sleeps. He can leave his bedroom windows open. He will wake up when the midnight wind blows against the musical instrument.

OLD JEW 2: But how are the separate parts to be recognized?

LYING JEW/ABRAHAM: In the first part the donkey is loud, in the second one the dog, in the third part you can hear a man and a woman speak with each other.

STANDING JEW/ISAAC: A man in the dark knows that the last part of the night has began when he hears a man and a woman speaking with each other.

LYING JEW/ABRAHAM: What is meant by a man and a woman speaking with each other?

STANDING JEW/ISAAC: What is meant by a man and a woman speaking with each other? It is the last part of the night.

LYING JEW/ABRAHAM: Why do they wait until the last part of the night to speak with each other?

STANDING JEW/ISAAC: Maybe they disagree about something when they go to bed and the first two parts of the night they're lying with their backs turned toward each other. Maybe one of them wakes up at the beginning of the third and deepest part of the night but isn't sure whether he's really awake and turns toward the other and touches her.

OLD JEW 2: In the light of the night?

OLD JEW 1: In the light that makes it clear that it is night but still shows what's happening.

OLD JEW 2: Black light mixed with white light?

OLD JEW 1: Tired light on light that thanks whomever it has woken up?

LYING JEW/ABRAHAM: Who loses proofs day and night?

OLD JEW 1: To conclude our performance we would like to stage a dance.

BENJAMIN: Rather not, please.

OLD JEW 1: The dance begins with the man who wants to stand on one leg while something is explained to him. He explains it again to others who stand on one leg and that's how the dance comes about.

(The two groups of old Jews become two dancing circles trying to dance through each other. Finally they stop, laughing and sweaty, and walk on to the camp's entrance gate. They lift the entrance gate from the ground and disappear with it.)

BENJAMIN: It is always terrible to see Jews dance, old or new. Jews never know when enough is enough. In the beginning there is formlessness and emptiness. Formlessness is like a thin green line enclosing the world. Darkness unfolds from that green line. Emptiness is like a small stone falling into a deep well. From emptiness arises water. From darkness comes light, from water land. Not all emptiness becomes water. A small terrifying part of emptiness remains. It has no name. The terrifying emptiness transforms into Jews and final emptiness. Half of the terrifying emptiness spits out Jews until it is depleted. The Jews are the replacements of the emptiness without the final emptiness. The final emptiness is the place where Isaac is tied up. The mountain is the temple mount. Isaac lies tied up in the temple's holy of holies. No one sees him there.

MAIMON: Immediately whole Jews, not first half ones?

BENJAMIN: What kind of emptiness is the emptiness that remains after a broken marriage? God thinks about the possibility that He's married to someone and that the marriage falls apart; what kind of emptiness remains after God has stopped thinking about this? God says to the angel: you are the angel of the Jew. The angel of the Jew says: It's me who determines who's a Jew.

MAIMON: A whole Jew?

BENJAMIN: The king of Egypt is an old man. Everyone who had attended his coronation has died. The crown princes die one by one and the king grows older and older. The king builds an underground grave for his sons and grandsons. The grave stretches further and further underground and the grave workers have to walk and crawl underground for hours to reach a place where they can work on a new burial chamber. Their eyes are red and their skin is dull and scaly. The king no longer wants to see anyone who has a bad skin. Anyone with skin disease has to leave Egypt immediately. Also anyone with blemishes on his skin or hair growing at an unusual place. Also anyone who could have forgotten that his skin is bad. The king decides that everyone who forgets easily will be banished from Egypt. The king's envoys are sent to all parts of the country to question whomever they meet. What is the name of your wife's father? The first time that you see your wife you know immediately that you want to marry her? When the envoy is unsatisfied with the answers he says that the questioned person has to leave Egypt. The questioned person asks what will happen to his wife and children. The envoy says that they may leave Egypt together with him. For months the envoys travel through the country. Some envoys become sick and lie in bed in remote villages and are unable to continue. In the desert beyond Egypt's border the group of skin disease patients and forgetful people is growing. They crowd together to protect themselves from the wind and the cold of the night. When something occurs in a story and it no longer seems necessary for understanding the story it is maybe the remainder of a memory.

MAIMON: Jews?

BENJAMIN: Whole Jews. A second story is an explanation of a first story but it doesn't make the first story more clear. Maybe the second story is the explanation of a third story but that explanation can only be given owing to the first story. Maybe the second story only remains an explanation of the first story out of gratitude or politeness toward the first story. A second story is an explanation of a first story. Which of the two is like a bride? Someone wants to tell the second story and says that the first story is more beautiful than any other story whatsoever. Someone writes a divorce letter and gives it to his wife. He is so ashamed that he is no longer able to tell a story or to listen to a story that is about a wedding. He cannot remarry or he can only marry if the wedding takes place without him having the intention to get married. And then? After his wedding he still cannot tell a story or listen to a story that is about a wedding. His wife doesn't talk about her wedding in his presence.

MAIMON: Why don't we all become non-Jews. Is that so difficult?

BENJAMIN: It is not as easy as a walk across a field. Someone is born as honorary Jew and gives the title away? A Jew in a joke asks all trees to take an oath that they will not injure him or testify against him but he always forgets one or two. The Jew asks one of the trees that he has forgotten for help. The tree lets him jump naked into a streaming river. When the Jew is back on dry land, cold and dripping from the water, the tree takes him into its arms. One time, two times, three times. And still the tree isn't sure that no remainder of Jew has been left in the Jew. The tree says: you embrace me like you're in the first week of mourning someone who isn't dead and I come on a mourning visit.

MAIMON: That's the joke?

BENJAMIN: Do you want a sequel joke for someone who doesn't immediately begin to laugh upon hearing the joke? The Jew from the joke thinks that he knows the way to the world to come. He invites the Jews to follow him. The Jews don't have time. A Jew says: of course I want to go to the world to come but now is not the right moment. He has promised his wife to eat with her in a restaurant, he has promised his children to play with them, he has promised a sick friend to visit him. Give him a couple of days, a couple of weeks more, and then he'll be ready to leave. The less time is left, the easier it becomes to make promises. The shrinking time becomes packed with promises? About what is someone still worried and by what is someone still distracted? Which joke still distracts a Jew? Which joke distracts a non-Jew? Which joke distracts an aged slave? The Jew from the joke makes a joke to delay his own departure. As long as it takes to tell a joke the Jews can take care of their business and fulfill their promises and the non-Jews can pack their luggage and join them too. A Jew may write his name in big letters on his suitcase so that he doesn't have to be worried that he won't be able to find his suitcase at the end of the journey. There is another story about the origin of the Jews. God invents the difference between Jews and non-Jews like a difference to deal with a contradiction in a text. God studies on his own. He has no one to discuss with. God is more afraid than anyone to encounter a contradiction. That's why God sometimes invents a difference before it is necessary. What can be done about it?

MAIMON: Is it easy to become a Jew?

BENJAMIN: As easy as a walk across a field. A Jew is sitting at a table in his garden, studying. The angel of death may not disturb him. The angel may climb a tree. The angel of death is the heaviest angel. He is heavier than the sun. If he climbs up a tree there is a big chance that the trunk will break in half. The Jew is scared by the sound and looks around. The angel of death may greet him. The angel of death cautiously enters a house where people are studying hard. He would like to explain a gesture or an exclamation as an invitation to study along with them and to forget why he has come in or to act as if has forgotten it. The angel of death hopes that he may stay in the house until it has become completely dark outside.

MAIMON: But if the angel of death has time to spare, may he visit one of the old goddesses?

BENJAMIN: Each day new angels are made. When an angel is made he can immediately sing. He sings an entire day and then he is pointed at. He doesn't have to be buried. Of each angel maybe a single drop of water remains. One day the anxious angels try to marry humans. They hope that they are allowed to live as long as the ones they're married to. At the end of the day it's raining heavier than ever before. Maybe the first angels continue to exist until the sixth day and the first angel is pointed at at the moment that the man and the woman are sent away from the garden. What do the angels sing? An angel looks at God to choose a song that is the most suitable to how He feels. But it is difficult to see how He feels and an angel is always worried and concerned. He's only got a short day. He'd rather not spend too much time thinking about what to sing. He begins to sing the first song that comes to his mind. He hears the angels around him sing other songs and he decides to sing along with the angel next to him but that angel at the same time decides to sing along with yet another angel. So the day passes without any angel singing a single song from beginning to end.

MAIMON: Can angels pray?

BENJAMIN: God hears something and doesn't know what it is. He asks the angel: is it a prayer? The angel doesn't dare to say no. God says: that was a beautiful prayer. I would like to hear it again. Can you find the one who said the prayer and bring him here? The angel asks: do you want me to ask the angel of death to bring him here? God says: can't you do it by yourself? The angel says: I'm not the angel of death. God says: I have a small request and that one small request you cannot even fulfill? An angel may take part in the heavenly assembly if there is an assembly on the angel's day. In the heavenly assembly the angels are the impatient ones and the dead Jews the patient ones. The dead don't want to be counted by the angels and the angels don't want to be counted by the dead. That's why it is impossible to determine who has the majority in the heavenly assembly. Deliberately damaged idols may also take part in the assembly. Some idols have broken fingers or a broken nose or empty eye sockets. The idols cannot speak or make any gestures when there is a vote. At the end of the day God points at all angels but He beckons one angel to come to Him. The remaining angel may help God clean up what the pointed-at angels have left: worn clothes and maybe crowns and other jewels that they have made themselves. The next day God tells the new angels: you want to live long? Look at him. He is more than a day old. The old angel is standing next to God and looks to the ground. God says: he feels like a little bird that's a bit confused. He can no longer sing. Maybe one of you wants to take care of him for the rest of this day? Also the angel of death is pointed at at the end of the day. The days look poorer and poorer but when does the angel of death have time to repair his day and make it more beautiful? A Jew doesn't have a study friend. On Friday morning his wife brings a large bucket of earth to his study. The whole day he kneads the earth but suddenly he notices that it has become evening and that the Sabbath has begun. He has made an incomplete angel. The angel has no voice. He cannot sing and he cannot study with someone else. The Jew says the evening prayer and welcomes the Sabbath. The incomplete angel sits on the ground and looks at him. The Jew points to his open mouth and makes an inviting gesture toward to the angel. He exits his study and the angel follows him to the dining room where the table has been set. The Jew asks his wife to set a plate and a glass for the angel. The Jew knows that the angel won't live longer than a day. The woman puts down a mattress for the angel on the floor of their bedroom. The Jew and his wife stay awake the whole night because the angel stays awake too. The next day the angel sits on a chair next to the Jew in his study. At the end of the day all three of them sit at the table but are unable to eat. It gets dark and they can no longer see each other's faces. The Jew says goodbye to the

Sabbath. The angel says goodbye to the Sabbath.

MAIMON: The angel has no voice; how does the angel say goodbye?

BENJAMIN: It is an incomplete angel.

MAIMON: Can you see from his facial expression that he is saying goodbye?

BENJAMIN: Maybe the angel waits until the scholar says goodbye and stands up next to him on his toes hopping up and down as if he is about to fly away. It is an incomplete angel. Maybe you can also see it from his facial expression.

MAIMON: That he is an incomplete angel? What kind of face does an angel have?

BENJAMIN: Someone says that an angel is only a face with wings. God has a thick book with portraits of angels who disappeared.

MAIMON: Is it allowed to make images of angels?

BENJAMIN: It is the only way in which He can remember individual angels. The angels He points at at the end of the day He forgets immediately. God opens the book at the point where the pages are still blank and invites the angel to read from the book. When the angel tries to read God suddenly shuts the book. The angel's face is squashed. The wings remain outside the book and continue to move for a moment. That's how God makes an imprint of the angel's face.

MAIMON: And God can remember the angel?

BENJAMIN: The image is a stain spread across two pages. Sometimes God asks an angel of a later day to look at the pages and to say what the stain reminds him of.

MAIMON: When the pages are not empty the angel doesn't have to be frightened?

BENJAMIN: God cannot sit still. He runs around and is noisy. The old goddesses no longer want to see God. They want to leave God in a completely dark place where they can never find Him again. An old goddess doesn't agree with this proposal. She suggests to leave God in a garden. No one knows anymore who this one old goddess is. The other old goddesses say that they agree with the new proposal but immediately afterward they all throw themselves onto the one old goddess and tear her apart into two halves. One half becomes the royal god of death and the other half the royal god of theater. The old goddesses make the royal god of death dig a grave for himself in a garden. The god of theater runs away crying and becomes a wanderer. He sleeps on porches, also the porches of temples built for him. The royal god of death and the royal god of theater still treat the old goddesses as if they're old goddesses themselves. The god of theater invites the old goddesses to appear. The god of death tries to touch them to find out whether they have really appeared.

MAIMON: Where are the other royal gods?

BENJAMIN: The king of the royal gods sleeps with a goddess, the daughter of another goddess. The daughter gets pregnant from the god of theater. The god of theater walks around like a small child and the other royal gods become afraid that he wants to embarrass them. Also his father and mother are afraid; only the god of death is not afraid. With toys the royal gods lure the child toward them. They gather around the child and when the child notices this it tries to escape. The royal gods easily stop it and holding it by its hands and feet pull it apart. They eat the torn-apart body parts. The daughter of the king of the royal gods snatches away the heart and brings it to her father. The king of the royal gods eats the heart and then sleeps with another goddess. The other goddess becomes pregnant and again gives birth to the god of theater. The other goddess is maybe the mother, maybe the daughter of the first goddess. The mother and daughter are played by old goddesses, so well that no one can guess which old goddess is playing whom. The god of death looks at the mother and the daughter. Suddenly he jumps up and grabs the daughter into his arms and carries her away. The mother says that she will make sure that the trees and plants will dry out and rot away if she doesn't get her daughter back. Humans and animals will starve. They will no longer bring sacrifices to the royal gods. The king of the royal gods asks the god of death to give back the daughter. The god of death says: she's married to me. I have given her something to eat and she has eaten it. You cannot just take her away from me. The king of the royal gods makes an agreement with the god of death. For four months of each year the daughter lives in the underworld being a good wife to god of death. The god of death is the god of theater's stepfather. The god of theater notices one day that he no longer feels impatient when he hears that a new play has been written. Because all good theater poets have died? The god of theater travels to the underworld. The dead are very busy preparing a theater festival. The dead theater poets don't write new plays. They rewrite their old plays to allow a performance by dead actors. In the underworld theater it is not possible to dance. The dead actors hardly have enough breath to pronounce short sentences. Instead of singing they can count slowly. The god of death welcomes the god of theater and asks him why he has come. The god of theater complains about the living poets. The god of death says that the god of theater may take along a poet from the underworld to the surface. The god of theater says: how can I choose? The god of death says: attend the performances, take your time, and make your choice.

In the theater you can sit between me and my wife. When someone thinks he is dying he sometimes asks someone else to stay with him and walk with him, out of the camp, and to continue to talk with him. That is also allowed. Finally the one who is dying lies down with his face toward the camp's fence as if with his face toward the only remaining wall.

MAIMON: And remains lying down like that.

BENJAMIN: And remains lying down as long as he can. Later he is buried. Everyone who has helped with the burial has to wash his hands afterward. The text of the law makes the hands unclean. He who has touched the text of the law has to wash his hands afterward. The text of the law makes unclean like the body of a dead person makes unclean. Only the text of the law kept in the temple and used by the priests does not make unclean. Otherwise the priests would constantly become unclean and they would be unable to behave like priests. Compare: the text of a play makes everyone who touches the text unclean except the actors. The scholars imitate priests who are afraid of uncleanliness because they would not be allowed to sacrifice. Or priests who reconstruct their temples day and night to clarify the movements of the sun and the moon and the stars to themselves. They move the altar to a place where the sun is setting at the end of the shortest day or where the light of the moon disappears at the end of the shortest night. The scholars who imitate the sky priests have no altars, neither inside temples nor in the open air. They play the moving of the altars by gathering in groups of ten men positioning themselves in such a way that the first light of the moon appears between two men standing side by side with their backs turned toward the light.

MAIMON: The text of any play makes unclean? The one of

a comedy too?

BENJAMIN: In the world to come anyone may act in any play. When an important non-Jew dies a death mask is made from his face. Long before he dies an actor has been selected who resembles him and who has practiced to walk just like him. The actor puts on the death mask and walks along in the funeral procession. Also the death masks of family members who died before are carried along, by less gifted actors. An important non-Jew is buried and several pairs of slaves fight with swords until one of each pair has died. The other slave doesn't get his freedom. At the next funeral he may fight again. The funeral guests look on and the masked actors do so too. Visiting the funerals of everyone someone knows takes a lot of time. Someone who is getting old and doesn't die is blamed even more if he skips the funeral of someone he knows.

MAIMON: Except when he says that he is seriously ill?

BENJAMIN: Except when he becomes a god. Someone notices that he's not dying and dresses up like a god so that he no longer needs to attend funerals.

(Jerusalem appears in the distance. It is late in the afternoon. The light becomes less bright. Benjamin and Maimon look at the city. A group of Jews comes from the direction of the city.)

BENJAMIN: Surrendering old Jews. Stalin hasn't come in time to save the city.

OLD JEW I: He says Stalin?

BENJAMIN: I say Stalin.

MAIMON: He says Stalin and I say Stalin. I'm sure you'd like to hear the latest news about Stalin.

OLD JEW I: Don't play jokes on us.

BENJAMIN: It's not a joke. Really.

MAIMON: Stalin is dead.

OLD JEW I: He said time.

MAIMON: Too late.

BENJAMIN: Do you think there's still time?

OLD JEW I: Stalin is dead?

MAIMON: Stalin is a dead Jew.

OLD JEW I: How should we believe this?

BENJAMIN: You're laughing?

OLD JEW I: No, I'm not laughing at all.

BENJAMIN: Do you think that this is a joke played on Jews?

OLD JEW I: Stalin is a Jew?

MAIMON: Has become.

BENJAMIN: According to the rules. A number of Jews surround him. They say: don't you know that the Jews feel that they don't receive a warm enough welcome anywhere? Then they ask him another time. And then another time. Stalin constantly nods his head as a sign that he has understood the question.

MAIMON: He dies as a result of the circumcision. The wound doesn't close. The blood continues to flow out. Stalin screams loudly. The circumciser pours wine over his hands but doesn't dare to stick one or more fingers into Stalin's mouth to quiet him down. The photo of his corpse is on the front page of today's Pravda. The photo occupies the entire front page. Stalin lies on his side on his bed, his face directed toward the closest wall, his eyes squeezed shut. If I had the newspaper with me I would have liked to show you. The rabbi of Birobizhan organizes the funeral. He is Stalin's most likely successor as secretary-general of the party. The rabbi is an acquaintance of mine. He is a Jew.

OLD JEW I: He is a Jew?

MAIMON: He will lose the war anyway.

OLD JEW I: Stalin is dead?

MAIMON: Stalin is sitting naked on a dark red pillow. Outside, in the glaring sun. It is midday. The witnesses stand around him in a circle. Inside the circle Stalin is sitting and the blind circumciser is standing, with the knife in one hand and in the other the bottle of sweet wine.

OLD JEW I: Stalin is naked?

MAIMON: His lower body is naked. His abdomen and his legs.

BENJAMIN: The circumciser is not blind; he squeezes his eyes shut and turns his face away.

MAIMON: The witnesses keep their eyes closed. Stalin closes his eyes before the circumciser touches him with the knife. Before he begins the circumciser offers Stalin a glass of the wine and Stalin empties the glass.

BENJAMIN: Good.

(The old Jews walk on. Jerusalem starts to burn.)

BENJAMIN: The city is already on fire. The walls are burning. Do you want to stand on the walls and hold a speech?

MAIMON: If that's expected of me.

BENJAMIN: By whom? By the old goddesses? They have already been disappointed so many times. They hardly care about one more time. You can address the city, saying that it no longer has to be worried. You can speak to it with a tender voice.

MAIMON: Do I have to speak?

BENJAMIN: You can also attack the city, at a gallop. Take good care of yourself. I don't believe that the city is still defended. Moreover, you're maybe one of those who receive permission to enter the city or even one of those who may always enter the city get permission and for whom they open the city gates when he approaches the city. And if the gates aren't wide enough the walls are broken down for him. Can you smell the burning city? Does it have a nice smell? Does it smell just?

MAIMON: I don't smell anything.

BENJAMIN: Maybe when you get closer. If you capture the city before it surrenders you are obliged at least to act as if you're pillaging it.

MAIMON: Pillaging what?

BENJAMIN: A pillager doesn't know precisely what he's looking for. That's why he is so often in a hurry and furious. He is afraid to notice afterward that he has overlooked the most worthy thing. Chests filled with jewelry, books full of text, beautiful slaves to set immediately free, maybe he is wasting his time and there are even more beautiful ones down the road.

MAIMON: How long does immediately take?

BENJAMIN: As long as it takes to pronounce a word.

MAIMON: How many old goddesses are there?

BENJAMIN: Not infinitely many. Otherwise it would be never dark at night and never light during the day. What are you waiting for? Until someone comes out to offer you the keys to the city? On the Sabbath it is prohibited to carry something from one place to another. But you're allowed to carry the clothes that you're wearing. How does a Jew open the front door of his house on the Sabbath? He has a key that is part of his clothing. A woman carries the key with her as an ornament, part of a necklace or a brooch, a man maybe carries it as a tie pin.

MAIMON: Is it Sabbath today?

BENJAMIN: What are you waiting for?

(Maimon walks toward the city. He disappears from sight. Soon after he reappears.)

BENJAMIN: That's fast.

MAIMON: The city is on fire.

BENJAMIN: What about the goddesses?

MAIMON: The goddesses are sitting in a room in the middle of the city. They are speaking with each other so intensely that they barely notice what is happening outside. Not even when the windows explode because of the heat from the flames. And not when I entered either.

BENJAMIN: You gave a speech?

MAIMON: No, I waved my arms a bit to get some attention. One of them asked whether I was angry because they had forgotten to invite me. I don't look like a goddess, right?

BENJAMIN: Most probably you didn't check well. Just a couple of women studying a text. If you had stayed they might have begun to study you.

MAIMON: The city is on fire and they don't pay attention.

BENJAMIN: What did you feel for them? What did they look like?

MAIMON: Do I look like a goddess?

BENJAMIN: If the old goddesses were your daughters, which one would you marry off first? How much time would you need between one wedding and the next? What does a world in which every act has to be loving look like?

MAIMON: Without being serious?

BENJAMIN: Sometimes yes, sometimes no. It's about ways of behaving, good manners. Or that every act has to be surprised or hospitable.

MAIMON: Why all the same?

BENJAMIN: Manners have to reinforce each other. Back and forth. Toward ever new heights. That is a form of politeness. How to greet someone? Extending a hand? The fingers spread out? In any case asking: how are you? And not expecting an answer. When you're not expecting an answer from someone always ask: how are you? Someone says something and you thank him because he says what you could have said. Out of politeness the border is blurred between what someone says and what is said about someone. As soon as someone asks you to do something you do it as well as possible. Without saying that something else might be better for you and for the other. You do it immediately. And if that's impossible? Then what? As if you didn't understand the question? Someone asks: may I feel this or that for you? How much time may you take to think about the question? May you take more time when you expect to say yes or when you expect to say no? You don't look someone straight in the face out of fear that the looking may be interpreted as a question. You don't stay awake where others are sleeping and you don't sleep where others are awake. For someone who is lost politeness is maybe the same thing as justice for a judge. What is polite is of course also determined by the manners of the majority. Someone may try to follow each rule of politeness that used to be customary. Someone is polite toward what may have been and toward what maybe yet will be. Someone is polite toward his feeling of the passage of time and toward his feeling of freedom. That is politeness that takes time. Finally, politeness is maybe about dignity. There we are, all of us, dignified as if we don't manage to end what we're doing by ourselves and also larger and more beautiful than expected. Someone says to someone else: what do you mean when you're looking at me like that?

(The old Jews reappear, dressed as goddesses. They form a semi-circle around Benjamin and Maimon.)

OLD JEW 1/GODDESS: May we now perhaps enjoy your performance?

MAIMON: What?

OLD JEW 1/GODDESS: We also performed for you.

BENJAMIN: Yet another play?

OLD JEW 1/GODDESS: No need. A performance. A conversation.

MAIMON: We didn't prepare anything.

OLD JEW 1/GODDESS: Really?

MAIMON: Really. We didn't know it would go like this.

OLD JEW 1/GODDESS: Mr. Benjamin, you certainly don't need any preparation?

BENJAMIN: I am nothing.

OLD JEW 1/GODDESS: Listen to him saying that he's nothing.

BENJAMIN: I am nothing.

OLD JEW 1/GODDESS: Listen who's saying that he's nothing. Do you see how it just happens, Mr. Maimon, please do join us.

MAIMON: I am nothing?

BENJAMIN: Look, a Jew with stars in his hair and he says he's nothing.

MAIMON: It is nothing.

OLD JEW 1/GODDESS: Here are twenty red roses, hand-picked.

MAIMON: It is nothing.

OLD JEW 1/GODDESS: Here are twenty selected carnations like twenty trembling birds in a tree.

BENJAMIN: Do you want to vote on something perhaps?

OLD JEW 1/GODDESS: What would we have to vote on?

Did you do something that would require a vote? Please, just continue your performance.

BENJAMIN: Maimon, do know anything?

MAIMON: What should we do?

OLD JEW 1/GODDESS: Is this still going somewhere?

MAIMON: How to do the end?

BENJAMIN: As if mourning is enough.

OLD JEW 1/GODDESS: Actually, why aren't you married?

BENJAMIN: I am married.

OLD JEW 1/GODDESS: We notice so little of it.

MAIMON: How to do the end?

BENJAMIN: Like a dancing Jew? Crying wildly?

MAIMON: Laughing wildly?

BENJAMIN: Wild Jew.

MAIMON: Leaves, feathers, seaweed in his hair.

BENJAMIN: Crown Jew.

MAIMON: Comfort Jew.

BENJAMIN: In a comfort bed.

MAIMON: If you want it it is not a dream.

BENJAMIN: Do I have to pinch your arm?

MAIMON: If a Jew feels it it is not a dream?

BENJAMIN: A Jew could think that he is the king of the end time.

MAIMON: If he didn't have the occasional nightmare.

OLD JEW 1/GODDESS: Sweet dream.

BENJAMIN: Sweet song.

OLD JEW 1/GODDESS: Comfort song.

BENJAMIN: A song in a song.

MAIMON: A Jew in a song.

BENJAMIN: When someone becomes a Jew because of a dream he remains a non-Jew.

MAIMON: When someone becomes a Jew and the end has already come?

BENJAMIN: A judge who thinks he's funny would say something like that.

MAIMON: A king who thinks he's funny.

BENJAMIN: A king has a son and appoints that son as his jester.

OLD JEW 1/GODDESS: Now what use is my feeling for what is funny?

BENJAMIN: A jester who isn't a judge has to be treated like a judge who has forgotten he is a judge?

OLD JEW 1/GODDESS: Can someone judge a life he hasn't lived himself?

MAIMON: Can someone judge a life as if he's a judge?

OLD JEW 1/GODDESS: Can someone judge a life as if he's not a judge?

BENJAMIN: Can a judge judge a life as if the judge is preparing a mourning speech?

OLD JEW 1/GODDESS: Can someone judge something that he's not mourning?

BENJAMIN: Can someone judge as if he decides how much someone may sleep and how far away someone has to be banished?

OLD JEW 1/GODDESS: Can someone mourn in advance and not want to be distracted?

MAIMON: Is someone inattentive when he wants to be distracted?

BENJAMIN: Someone wakes up and speaks and it becomes dark?

MAIMON: Does usage in dreams count?

BENJAMIN: Someone who's dying crawls to the entrance of a slaughterhouse and says that he wants to take the place of one of the animals.

MAIMON: The butchers asks: which animal?

BENJAMIN: What is the most usual animal?

OLD JEW I/GODDESS: What is the most inattentive animal?

MAIMON: What is a Jew forever?

BENJAMIN: He walks on the street and acts as if he no longer can go on.

MAIMON: Exhausted gestures in nearly exhausted light?

BENJAMIN: Saying a blessing?

MAIMON: What should we do?

BENJAMIN: Begin at the beginning.

MAIMON: It's not easy.

BENJAMIN: It's not as easy as a chicken's walk across a field.

MAIMON: How to do the beginning?

BENJAMIN: As if it's not real.

MAIMON: How to do the end?

BENJAMIN: As if someone has made an agreement with someone to celebrate something the day after, except when the end has happened before.

OLD JEW I/GODDESS: To celebrate what?

BENJAMIN: As if the world has had enough of the days.

MAIMON: And stops spinning.

BENJAMIN: In one part of the world it is always light and in one part always dark.

MAIMON: In a strip from north to south there is dawn and in another strip there is dusk and a dark red sun.

BENJAMIN: It is the morning and the afternoon of the Sabbath where it is always light and the evening and the night of the Sabbath where it is always dark.

MAIMON: The chicken is standing upright in the elongated strip and stares at the dark red sun.

BENJAMIN: Egg laying chicken or table chicken?

MAIMON: Patient chicken or impatient chicken?

BENJAMIN: Patient enough to distinguish day and night?

MAIMON: A chicken is standing in a field and no one can

hear it scream.

BENJAMIN: A wolf is shocked because it has swallowed all words.

MAIMON: They were sweet.

BENJAMIN: Like stones?

MAIMON: Stars or nightly screams?

BENJAMIN: Burning stones?

MAIMON: Sleeping Jew or non-sleeping Jew?

BENJAMIN: Someone gets a kiss meant for someone else.

MAIMON: Justice sleep?

BENJAMIN: Beauty sleep?

MAIMON: Life and health?

BENJAMIN: Someone touches someone who has touched a dead body.

MAIMON: How to do a sunset?

BENJAMIN: As if it's real. As if a wolf swallows the sky. First the chickens, then the sky.

MAIMON: A Jewish wolf?

BENJAMIN: A Jewish wolf that is afraid that someone wants to cut it open to find something back.

MAIMON: How to do the end?

BENJAMIN: A Jewish wolf takes a bath, eats with its wife and children, goes to sleep next to its wife, wakes up the next morning, is happy.

MAIMON: How to do a Jew?

BENJAMIN: How to do a Jew who's cold?

MAIMON: Do like a Jew?

BENJAMIN: How to do two Jews?

MAIMON: How to do two Jews?

BENJAMIN: Once you've done one Jew you've done them all.